Ghoulish Games
&
Other Eerie Tales

Ghoulish Games
&
Other Eerie Tales

*After tonight, visiting the cemetery
will never be the same!*

Plaxton Emmons

iUniverse, Inc.
New York   Bloomington

Ghoulish Games & Other Eerie Tales

After tonight, visiting the cemetery will never be the same!

Copyright © 2010 by Plaxton Emmons

iUniverse books may be ordered through booksellers or by contacting:
iUniverse
1663 Liberty Drive
Bloomington, IN 47403
www.iuniverse.com
1-800-Authors (1-800-288-4677)

Because of the dynamic nature of the Internet, any Web addresses or links contained in this book may have changed since publication and may no longer be valid. This is a work of fiction. All of the characters, names, incidents, organizations, and dialogue in this novel are either the products of the author's imagination or are used fictitiously.

ISBN: 978-1-4502-4295-0 (pbk)
ISBN: 978-1-4502-4296-7 (ebk)

Printed in the United States of America
iUniverse rev. date: 7/30/10

DEDICATION

I'd like to dedicate this book "Ghoulish Games & Other Eerie Tales" to the memory of three of my friends who tragically lost their lives while they were still young:

Stephen Lee
(December 4, 2003)

Terry Davis
(December 29, 2006)

Nick Mangarcina
(November 22, 2007)

GONE BUT NOT FORGOTTEN

Contents

FOREWORD

The following poems and stories came by reading, research, and observing. I find this funny; the ideas of "The House of Gomorrah Falls" came to me when I was reading Ernest Hemingway's The Old Man and the Sea. I don't know why because the story has nothing to do with fishing at all. I began thinking about my female Siberian husky that killed possums that came into my yard during the night. Then I remembered a vacation to Baltimore several years before that. While I was there, I tried my best not to say y'all to those people. I went to Poe's house, which isn't far from his grave at Westminster Cemetery, perhaps one of America's most haunted cemeteries. I got the ideas for "Eerie October" and one poem from researching Westminster Cemetery.

Cemeteries can be scary places. I'd heard and read of several of them leading to the gates of hell. According to what I read about one cemetery in Kansas, one woman, who was buried there, was hanged after convicted of witchcraft. According to legend, she conceived a child with Satan. Many people have also witnessed horribly vicious demons in the cemetery as well and say that it's best if anyone stays away from it. To get to a conclusion, I believe that ghosts, ghouls, goblins, and witches have been terrorizing America long before Islamic terrorists.

-Plaxton Emmons

THE SISTERS OF WITCHES' GALLOWS LANE

Although the most acute judges of the witches and even the witches themselves, were convinced of the guilt of witchery, guilt nevertheless was nonexistent. It thus with all-guilt.
Friedrich Nietzsche

PROLOG

It was a black night on October 30, 1700, when 16-year-old triplet sisters Martha, Melinda, and Miranda Kale stood before a mammoth crowd after the Judge Silas Hooker had convicted them of witchcraft and sentenced them to death. As the furious crowd's screams grew louder, their mother Deborah Kale wept over their father Jonah's shoulder. After the girls were dead, their corpses were buried by the hill where stood the tree from which they were hanged. For over 300 years, the place for the people of Bethel's Hollow, Mississippi, was infamous as "Witches' Gallows Lane."

THE DREADFUL DEATH OF VANESSA LONDON

The bell rang at three on the afternoon of Friday, May 6, 2005. All the juniors and seniors at Bethel's Hollow High School had one thing on their minds: the prom. For Kermit Frost, he had more than the prom. He was putting his blue Volkswagen in reverse as he repeatedly recited to himself what he was planning to ask his high-school love.

"Vanessa Marie London, will you be my wife?"

He also had a sapphire-diamond ring that he'd bought at Bethel Square Mall a day earlier.

Four hours later, he was listening to Clint and Lisa Black sing "When I Said, I Do" on the radio as he drove to Vanessa's house.

"I want this to be our song," he thought.

He drove into her yard and got out of the car. After he rang the doorbell, Vanessa walked outside. She had her long, blond hair down. She was wearing a strapless, dark-blue dress and dark-blue high heels. She was smiling as she asked, "Are you ready for tonight?"

"Sweetheart, I've been ready for this night since the morning of November 24, 1986."

"Oh, Kermit!"

"Vanessa Marie London," he sighed.

"Yes, Kermit Aaron Frost."

"You know, we've been dating since September 1, 2001."

"We sure have," she said with her Southern drawl.

He pulled the ring from the pocket of his blue coat and heard her whisper, "Yes!"

"You will marry me?"

"I will."

They walked to the car. After Kermit sat behind the wheel, he drove to the high school.

When they walked inside the multipurpose building, they heard Gilda Wagner blurt out, "Kermit! Vanessa!"

They turned to see her with Kyle Wright. She hugged Vanessa and told her, "You look so pretty!"

"So do you, Gilda!"

"How's it going, Kermit?" Kyle asked.

"I'm great. Vanessa and I are engaged."

"Are you serious?"

"I'm cemetery-dead serious! I proposed today!"

"Congratulations."

Suddenly, the deejay played the Righteous Brothers' "Unchained Melody."

"Kermit, I love this song!" Vanessa told him.

He took her hand and walked her to the dance floor. Kyle and Gilda did the same as well as his best friend Walter Robeson and his high-school love Danielle Davis. As the two were slow-dancing, Kermit said, "Vanessa."

"Yes, Kermit."

"I'd like for us to go somewhere after we leave here at midnight. Just me and you."

"Where's that?"

"Witches' Gallows Lane."

"Won't we get arrested for going down there?"

"That's only if the police catches us."

"Only if you wanna go," she sighed.

"That's my girl!"

Prom ended at midnight. Kermit and Vanessa went toward Witches' Gallows Lane and recognized a wooden sign that had red, large letters that read:

WARNING:

ANYONE CAUGHT ON THIS PROPERTY WITHOUT PERMISSION WILL BE ARRESTED FOR TRESPASSING!

NO EXCEPTIONS!

NO JOKE!

"Who gives a rat's ass?" Kermit thought. "I believe those are only legends."

"What legends?" Vanessa wondered.

"Those Kale girls have been dead for centuries. They have more fried brain-cells than Ozzy Osbourne for Christ sake! There's no way they're gonna rise from their graves and curse us with leprosy or some horrible-spell bullshit like that."

He drove down the curvy lane as "Highway to Hell" by AC/DC was on the radio.

"This seems like the road to hell," Vanessa thought.

One mile later, Kermit was still driving. Then he saw the hill. He put the car in park and turned the ignition off. They both got out and saw that the place had a very despairing atmosphere. It was dead silent-not even crickets chirping. It sounded like an ancient tomb that hadn't been entered in thousands of years. It didn't feel like May for Southern Mississippi at all. It actually felt like Northern Vermont in December.

"Damn, this place is weird," Vanessa thought.

Kermit looked to the stone steps and dared to jog up the hill. When he got up there, three ropes fell from the branches of the tree. There were cobras wrapped around the loops in the ropes.

"Holy shit!" he screamed.

He ran down the steps. He was out of breath when he told Vanessa, "Damn, that was evil!"

"I agree! Let's get outta here! Now!"

Then a gunshot was heard. Vanessa became decapitated. After her body fell to the ground, Kermit saw a bald midget standing behind where she was standing. His face reminded Kermit of when he'd seen Lon Chaney as Quasimodo in The Hunchback of Notre Dame years earlier. He wore a gray sweater and blue jeans along with brown boots. In his hand, he was holding a rifle.

"Get outta here while you still can, boy!" he snarled, then fired his gun into the air.

Kermit blinked his eyes and saw the midget gone. He dialed the police and waited until Officer George Thompson drove down there.

"What the hell do you think you're doing coming down here after midnight?"

Thompson, a Vietnam veteran and a former drill sergeant in the US Army, was furious.

"I," Kermit started.

Thompson interrupted by shouting, "Did you not read the sign up there? Or are you just completely ill fucking literate?"

"Mr. Thompson."

"I oughta arrest your ass for trespassing!"

"I called to report a homicide."

Thompson looked down to see Vanessa's corpse.

"Holy Jesus!"

Then he looked to Kermit and calmly told him, "Son, you're lucky I don't arrest you. What I want you to do right now. I don't care where you go. But get in your vehicle and leave this place, promising me you'll never come back here if you're alive a million years from tonight."

"Yes, sir."

MARTHA

Kyle and Gilda were at the graveyard behind the church as they placed red roses on the gravestone that read:

VANESSA MARIE LONDON

DEC 9 1986

MAY 7 2005

BELOVED DAUGHTER

It was the night of what would've been Vanessa's nineteenth birthday. The two were in Kyle's car when they left the graveyard. When he got near Witches' Gallows Lane, he and Gilda saw a blond girl dressed in a red robe as she stood by it.

"Maybe we should stop and ask if she'd like a ride," Gilda said.

The girl vanished when Kyle stopped.

"That was creepy," Gilda thought.

"No shit!"

"I wonder if that was one of the Kale girls," Gilda thought.

"I wouldn't wanna know."

"Kyle, do you believe in ghosts?"

"I guess you could say that."

"I believe that a soul can never come back once it enters heaven or hell. But the spirit may stay here as long as it wants."

"Makes sense."

Kyle drove into Gilda's front yard.

"What do you wanna do tomorrow?" she asked.

"I guess we can meet at the library in the morning."

"Great."

It was around ten the next morning when Kyle and Gilda sat at a table in the library. She was looking at a book about medieval Europe. Ms. Barbara Stone, her English teacher, had given the class a choice of a five-page paper on the Dark Age or a project on the Roman Empire for their final exam because she had them study King Arthur and William Shakespeare's Julius Caesar. Then Gilda recognized Danielle walk in with a blond girl standing at five-eight. She was wearing a black shirt of Johnny Cash under a brown, fur coat and Calvin Klein jeans along with cowboy boots. She and Danielle walked to where Kyle and Gilda were sitting.

"Hey, y'all," Danielle told them.

"Hey," Gilda said.

"I'm Dana, y'all," the girl said in a heavily Southern accent.

"This is my cousin," Danielle told them.

"I'm from Tennessee."

"Awesome," Gilda thought.

"I'm planning to attend Ole Miss in January."

"We have a friend who's at Ole Miss. He wants to be an art teacher."

"What's his name?" Dana asked.

"Kermit Frost."

"A combination of Kermit the Frog and the poet Robert Frost," Dana thought.

"You're good!" Kyle laughed.

Then Gilda's cell phone rang. She saw that it was Kermit calling. She eagerly answered by saying, "Hello."

"Excuse me, ma'am," Mrs. Ruth Jones, the head of the library staff, said as she approached the table.

"You need to go outside with that phone."

"Sorry," Gilda whispered.

She listened to Kermit talk as she walked outside.

"Well, Danny has this cousin. Dana's her name."

"Dana's a pretty name," he thought.

"I knew you'd say that."

"Is she seeing anyone?"

"I'll ask her. By the way, where are you right now?"

"I'm at my house."

"That's awesome!"

"I made it home last night."

"I guess we can bring her over tonight so y'all two can meet. "

"That'll be fantastic."

"Okay. We'll see you at around seven, I guess."

"Bye, Gilda."

Gilda hung up and walked back inside the library.

"Dana, are you seeing anyone back at home?" she asked.

"Well, me and my boyfriend just broke up last month. So, no."

"I just talked to Kermit about you."

"Really?"

"We're gonna bring you to meet him tonight."

"I'd love that."

"Well, we'll see y'all later," Danielle told them.

In her car, Danielle told Dana, "Kermit was gonna marry his high-school sweetie. Vanessa was her name. They went to Witches' Gallows

Lane after the prom. That was when she was murdered. It's been hell for him."

"She was murdered?"

"He said he saw who did it. He didn't wanna explain it to the cop because he thought he'd be sent to the loon house."

"Sounds like a scary place."

"I defiantly agree."

"I feel so bad for him."

"Vanessa was a good girl. She went to church a lot. Because she was a real Christian. She didn't drink or smoke at all. She was a cheerleader. But not like most of the cheerleaders at our school. She wasn't rude or preppy. She didn't walk with her nose to the air. She was elected 'Sweetest Female Student' in her freshman and sophomore year. She and Kermit were elected Prom King and Queen. Then she died just after that. But she's in a much better place."

Danielle turned the radio up to hear John Lennon and Yoko Ono along with the Harlem Community Choir and thought, "She's in a much better place than this world that's being torn apart by that damn war. There's hope there."

She was thinking of the wars in Afghanistan and Iraq. Then Dana thought, "Now, I understand what Plato meant when he said that only the dead have seen the end of the war."

"I see what you mean. Plato's been dead over 2,000 years. And the world was torn apart by war back in his time."

"I believe the world's been torn apart by war ever since Lucifer was cast from heaven."

"Good point."

Hours later, they were on Kermit's front porch. After it got very quiet, Dana dared and asked, "Kermit what do you know about Witches' Gallows Lane?"

He spat the beer from his mouth and dropped his bottle of Bud Light and his cigarette.

"What the hell did you just ask me?"

"Witches' Gallows Lane. Is it as haunted as people believe?"

"Damn right! That place is fucking evil!"

Tears began running down his face.

"Kermit, I am so sorry!" Dana swore.

"Don't worry about it!" he snapped, having his hands over his face.

Dana dialed Kermit's number at midnight.

"Hello," he answered.

"Hey, Kermit. This is Dana Wallace, Danielle Davis's cousin."

"Hi! How are you?"

"I'm doing fine. I was wondering what you wanted to do today."

He sighed and said, "I don't know."

"I'd love to go to Bethel Square Mall."

"Nice," he thought.

"You want to?"

"Sure!"

"Great! I love that Mexican cuisine in their food court."

"I love Enrique's, too!"

Then Dana changed the subject by saying, "Kermit, tell me about yourself."

"I was born in Hattiesburg, Mississippi, on November 24, 1986. I was born on Ted Bundy's fortieth birthday."

"That's scary."

"That's what I said."

"I was born in North Carolina on February 12, 1987. I have the same birthday as Abraham Lincoln and Charles Darwin."

"Well, my favorite color's blue."

"I love blue. But my favorite color's green."

"Do you have a favorite book?"

"In fact, I do. It's Bram Stoker's Dracula."

"So, you're a vampire fan, I guess."

"Yes! I've read all Ann Rice's vampire books. I've read Salem's Lot by Stephen King in less than a week."

"My favorite author is Edgar Allan Poe. I loved 'The Tell-Tale Heart.' "

"You have a favorite movie, Kermit?"

"South Park: The Movie. That was hilarious!"

"It was."

"Tell me about your favorite celebrities."

"I love Jennifer Love Hewitt! I've seen all her movies. I told you that I'm a vampire fan. So, I've seen Bela Lugosi in all those vampire movies he did."

"I'm a fan of the Chicago Bulls. Dennis Rodman's my favorite."

"I can't stand him. He is disturbing."

"And I love music by Nirvana. I like some country music. Especially Hank Williams, Jr."

"I love Kurt Cobain. And Hank Junior. I know we country folks can survive."

"Well, what are you doing in the meantime, Dana?"

"I don't know."

"Well, I'll see you at the food court in the mall at around twelve."

At around noon, Dana ordered a monster chimichanga with chicken and shrimp from Enrique's at the food court in Bethel Square Mall.

"Okay. I'll bring it out to you round fifteen minutes," Antonio, the young hombre, told her from behind the counter.

"Muchos gracias, Senor Antonio."

"No problemo," he said, smiling.

"You know Spanish?" Kermit guessed, sneaking up to her.

She quickly turned around to see him and said, "Kermit! What a surprise!"

"I told you I'd be here. Said around noon, right?"

"Yeah. So, what do you want to eat? It's all on me."

"I want a monster beef-burrito with cheese."

"Monster beef-burrito with cheese?" Antonio guessed.

"Si, senor."

He and Dana went to a table and sat.

"I gotta call someone," he told her.

"Who?"

"Dr. Roger Clark. I've been seeing him in Oxford."

"What kind of doctor?"

"Psychologist."

He dialed Dr. Clark's cell phone and heard him answer the second ring.

"Hello."

"Dr. Clark, this is Kermit Frost."

"How are you, Kermit?"

"I met someone new. And I'm eating lunch with her right now."

"I'm very proud."

"I'm proud of myself as well."

"What's her name?"

"Dana."

"I like that name."

"I like it, too."

"Okay, Dr. Clark. You take care."

"You, too, Kermit. Hope to see you soon."

"Later."

After he hung up, he heard Martha Kale's voice inside his head.

"Don't count on it to last for long, Kermit!"

"Holy shit!" he shrieked, jumping from the table.

"What's wrong, Kermit?" Dana asked.

"I think I heard Martha Kale!"

"Who?"

"Martha Kale! One of the sisters who were convicted as a witch here in Bethel's Hollow in 1700!"

"Well, let's go."

The two ran out to the parking lot.

"Stop running!" a security guard yelled.

They ignored him and ran to their cars. They sped away after that. Then the officer felt Martha tap his shoulder.

"What the hell you want, girl?"

She snapped her fingers and said, "Prepare for The Mandrill with Volcanic Breath."

A winged mandrill having dark-red fur flew from the air and exhaled fire onto the officer who was running for his life. Everyone ran out there to see what'd happened. The mandrill flew behind all the horrified people and blew fire onto them. Nearly a hundred people were burned to death. Fire engines zoomed to the scene and sprayed the fires.

Kermit was still on the way home, listening to Elton John sing "Step into Christmas" on the radio when it was interrupted.

"There's been a fire at Bethel Square Mall just minutes ago. The police have counted ninety-eight bodies of people who died in the fire."

Then he turned the radio off to hear his mom Wanda Frost calling.

"Hello!"

"Kermit! Thank God!"

"I know, Mom. I'm fine."

"Okay."

"I'm coming."

"That'll be good."

When he got home, he dialed Dana's cell number.

"Hello," she answered the second ring.

"Dana?"

"Yes."

"Did you hear the radio?"

"I just heard. Ninety-eight people were killed in that fire."

"It's a horrible tragedy."

"I agree."

"I hope they find out how the fire started."

Then Kermit heard Father Henry Kennedy beeping in.

"Dana, I'll call you back. Someone's calling me right now."

"Bye."

He answered Father Kennedy's call.

"Hello."

"Kermit?"

"Yes, Father Kennedy."

"I called to tell you that Martha Kale's been unleashed from her grave at Witches' Gallows Lane. It is she who's responsible for the fire. She and her fiendish pet mandrill. The Mandrill with Volcanic Breath."

"A mandrill?"

"It's a type of ape."

"Thanks for the information."

"Kermit, I need you to come to my office at the church."

"Okay."

Kermit walked into Father Kennedy's office.

"Kermit, I'm glad to see you."

"What do you have for me?"

He held out a glassed bottle of water and said, "Martha Kale is a vicious demon employed by Satan as we speak. You'll need this to guide you as you send her back to hell."

"Thank you."

"Good luck," Father Kennedy said. "And may the grace of our Lord Jesus Christ be with you."

"Yes, sir."

When Kermit got to his car, he dialed Dana's number.

"Hello."

"Dana, I just found out from a priest what started the fire."

"What?"

"It was Martha Kale and her pet mandrill that breathes fire."

"What the hell's a mandrill?"

"It's a type of ape."

"That's weird."

"I didn't say it wasn't."

"That bitch has to be stopped."

"I'm glad you said that. Because Father Henry Kennedy gave me a bottle of holy water."

"What's holy water gonna do?"

"She's a damn demon for Christ sake! And I think we should go down Witches' Gallows Lane together."

"You and me?"

"Yes, Dana! it's an evil place!"

"I'll go with you," she sighed.

It was around midnight when Dana rode with Kermit down Witches' Gallows Lane.

"The reason that this place is named what it is is triplet sisters Martha, Melinda, and Miranda Kale were convicted of their crimes of witchcraft by the Judge Silas Hooker in the year 1700. Then he gave them the death penalty. They were hanged down here. It's only been visited several times. Vanessa and I came down here on the night of our senior prom. Hadn't it been for you, I still wouldn't have forgiven myself."

"Vanessa died down here that night. Gruesomely."

He drove down the lane until he saw the hill. He saw an apparition of Vanessa standing up there. She was gone in the blink of an eye. Dana got out of the car and asked Kermit, "Did you just see that ghost?"

"Actually, I knew her when she was living. I saw her almost every day for years."

They heard the car violently explode after that. They looked to see the winged mandrill in the air. Kermit twisted the cap from the bottle.

"Sling that on me if you think you're that tough, Kermit!" the mandrill snarled.

"I am that tough!"

When he threw the water, it hit the mandrill's face. The horrible fiend screamed in pain as it fell to the ground and died.

"You son of a bitch!" Martha screamed from behind Kermit.

He and Dana turned around to see her.

"You killed my pet!"

"You're next!" Dana told her.

Kermit threw the bottle and struck Martha's forehead. She screamed bloody murder as she melted.

Martha Kale was nevermore.

MELINDA

Kermit's dad Bill Frost woke him up at around seven a.m.

"You have a phone call."

He took the phone from his dad's hand.

"Hello."

"Kermit," Father Kennedy said from the other line.

"Good morning, Father Kennedy. I have great news: thanks to me, Martha Kale is no more."

"Excellent. But don't get that comfortable because you'll now have to watch for her sister Melinda and her cobras. And she means business."

"Thanks for the warning."

"You're most welcomed."

The two hung up. Kermit blinked his eyes and saw a stranger in his room. She had long, red hair and wore a violet robe. There was a black cobra sitting on her shoulder.

"Melinda Kale!" he said.

"How dare you?"

"I'll get you next!"

"You don't have what it takes, Kermit."

"I'll have to see to that."

"Take a look around. You're already dead. You've just made it to hell."

When he looked around, he found himself surrounded by black cobras. One took a chunk of his heel and caused him to scream bloody murder. Bill and Wanda found their dead son surrounded by cobras and Melinda gone when they got to the room. Bill ran back to their room and got his rifle. He shot them all dead when he got back.

It was that afternoon when Danielle was getting out of school for the day. She heard her cell phone ring. She answered it and said, "Hello."

"Danielle! It's horrible!"

"What happened, Dana?"

"I'm sorry I waited so long to tell you. But they found Kermit this morning! They found him in his bedroom, surrounded by cobras!"

"What the hell? Do they know how they got in there with him?"

"No."

"That's very weird."

"Well, I'll talk to you when you get home, Danielle."

"Bye."

When she was on the way home, Father Kennedy called Danielle.

"Hello."

"Danielle!"

"Hi, Father."

"I know that it was Martha's sister Melinda who killed Kermit. She put those cobras in that room with him."

"How will anyone else believe that?"

"Let them deny what they wish. But they'll wish that they didn't as they're burning in hell."

Two days later, Father Kennedy stood before Kyle, Walter, Calvin Frost, and Evan Frost as they carried Kermit's corpse in a black casket from a black hearse to the gravesite. After Father Kennedy prayed over the grave, everyone walked toward the gate. Then he recognized Kyle and Gilda and ran to them.

"Kyle! Gilda!"

"Yes, Father," Gilda answered.

"You are in grave danger."

Kyle didn't understand at first. He turned to Gilda and asked, "What's he saying?"

Dana approached them and said, "I know exactly what he's saying."

When they turned to her, she said, "She's Martha's sister. And she wants revenge for her. We're all lucky to be alive. Very lucky."

"How do you know this, Dana?" Gilda asked.

"I was with Kermit when he killed Martha at Witches' Gallows Lane. And I had a good clue who the next sister would kill first."

"I get her drift," Kyle said.

Then they felt cold raindrops on them as a dark cloud rolled over them.

"We need to go!" Gilda said.

It suddenly began pouring rain. Walter was riding with Danielle as he lit a cigarette and sighed, "I'm gonna miss Kermit. In fact, I already miss him so much."

"I do, too," Danielle said.

"What was that about him slaying an evil witch?" Walter asked.

"Forget about it. Get the Kale Witches outta your mind!"

Not a syllable was spoken until Danielle got to Walter's house.

"See ya tomorrow," she told him.

"Bye."

They kissed each other's lips. Walter went inside his house, hurrying out of the cold rain. The next day was Thursday, December 15, 2005. Veronica, Gilda's mom, told her, "I need to do my Christmas shopping."

"I was thinking the same thing," Gilda said.

She called Dana and Danielle and asked them, "How would y'all like to go Christmas shopping?"

"Today?" Dana asked.

"Today! Now!"

"Let me ask Dana."

"Well, let me know."

"I'll ask her right quick."

"Go ask her."

"Hold on."

She asked Dana and heard her reply yes. She went back and told Gilda, "She said yes."

"Okay! Let's go!"

At the graveyard, two friends were placing flowers at Kermit's grave. Then they saw Melinda standing at the corner, holding a cobra.

"Do you know her?" the blond asked the brunette.

"I'm glad I don't."

Melinda met them at the gate. She released the cobra onto them. It began biting both of the girls. The residents ran to see the girls' bodies but Melinda nor the snake anywhere in sight. The police pronounced them as Dead at the Scene. An elderly woman blurted out, "Them girls knew Kermit Frost!"

"Who?" Thompson asked.

"The boy who was said to of died from the evil curse at Witches' Gallows Lane! They buried him here yesterday!"

"No fucking way!"

Thompson looked to the other officers and said, "I want you to guard Witches' Gallows Lane. Arrest anyone who walks any less than ten feet from it!"

He turned to the others and said, "I want y'all to stay and guard this graveyard. Make sure not a soul enters that gate! I don't give a rat's ass if they have permission from the President!"

"Yes, sir!"

When they got in front of Witches' Gallows Lane, they saw Melinda there.

"Ma'am, we're gonna have to arrest you for trespassing," one officer told her.

She threw the cobra from her shoulder onto him. It bit his face and caused him to fall to the ground. He was dead in a matter of seconds.

"That's it, bitch!" the other officer swore.

Melinda had another cobra by her feet without him knowing. It rose up and bit his knee. He screamed bloody murder. He also died.

When the seven o'clock news came on, the local reporter announced that Bethel's Hollow Police suspect that a serial killer was on the loose and they were offering a $5000 reward for his or her capture. Danielle's cell phone rang. She answered Walter's call by saying, "Hello."

"Hey, Danielle."

"Hi, Walter," she sighed.

"Did you hear? Two cops were killed at Witches' Gallows Lane today!"

"I just heard. They were bit to death by cobras. I wonder how they got there. Cobras are of Africa, aren't they?"

"That's what I heard about them."

Then she heard him scream a bloodcurdling scream because of one of Melinda's cobras biting him. On the other line, she heard Melinda snarl, "Walter has to go now."

Danielle hung up and screamed, "Walter!"

"What happened to Walter?" Dana asked.

"The witch Melinda got him!"

"Oh, no!"

Danielle dialed Gilda's number and heard her answer the second ring.

"Hello."

"Gilda! It's horrible!"

"What?"

"Walter's dead!"

"What the hell?"

"We were talking on the phone when I heard him scream bloody murder. Then some sicko came on the line and made me feel threatened. I'm sure it was Melinda Kale, the witch."

"That bitch has to be stopped!"

"What do we do?"

"Crucifix? Holy water? Hell if I'd know!"

"Kermit killed Martha by holy water," Dana said.

Danielle thought of an idea. After a while, she dialed the police and told the receptionist, "I need to go down Witches' Gallows Lane!"

"What the hell are you talking about?" the receptionist snapped.

"I know how to kill the evil curse on that place."

"Hold, please."

A minute later, Thompson came to the phone and said, "George Thompson speaking."

"This is Danielle Davis. I need permission to go down Witches' Gallows Lane. I know how to destroy the evil curse on that place."

"I'm sure people have been saying that shit for centuries. But I bet you're thinking just like them."

"I promise!"

"Sure, you do."

He hung up. Danielle hung the phone up and growled. At the police department, Thompson turned around and saw Melinda standing in front of him. She was holding a cobra.

"What the hell?"

He pulled his pistol out. Before he could pull the trigger, the cobra took a chunk of his hand. He screamed as he fell to the floor. The receptionist called an ambulance for him. When she looked back, she saw that Melinda was gone.

"Looks like we've seen the killer," she told one officer.

"Now, she's a wanted fugitive with a $5000 reward on her head."

"That little girl was right!" the receptionist snapped.

"What little girl?"

"Danielle Davis, she said her name was."

"I better go to her house and ask her questions."

Minutes later, Barry Davis, Danielle's dad, heard the doorbell ring. He answered it and saw two officers standing there.

"Good evening. I need to have some words with Ms. Danielle Davis."

"What's she done?"

"Get her for me immediately!"

"Yes, sir."

Dana and Danielle walked into the room and saw the officers.

"What's going on?" Danielle asked.

"Aren't you Danielle Davis?" one of the officers asked.

"Yes, sir."

"Step outside with us. We need to ask you some questions."

She and Dana walked outside with the officers.

"What do you know about Kermit Frost being killed by the evil curse at Witches' Gallows Lane?"

"Everything!" Dana blurted out.

"Who are you?"

"I'm Dana Wallace, Danielle's cousin. I was with him when he was down there and slew that evil witch. It's a very long story."

"Well, we just saw someone at the station. She used a cobra to kill Officer George Thompson. We think you'd know something about her."

"That was Melinda Kale," Danielle told him. "She's the first witch's sister. After Kermit killed the first witch, she rose from her grave and killed him. And she's killed seven other people."

"And I believe you were dating Walter Robeson, whom was just murdered tonight. Am I correct?"

"That's right. We were gonna get married next fall."

The officer got on his walkie-talkie and said, "I talked with the Davis girl. She said she was Robeson's fiancée. She says that he was killed by the curse at Witches' Gallows Lane, too."

"Drive her down there. And tell her we apologize."

"Yes, sir!"

He looked to the girls and told them, "Y'all, we're going to Witches' Gallows Lane. They owe you an apology."

When they were driving down Witches' Gallows Lane, it felt like thirty-below zero for the officers and the girls.

"Damn, this place is weird," one officer thought.

They all got out of the car. At first, Melinda was nowhere to be seen.

"Melinda!" Dana called. "We know you're around!"

She appeared before them.

"I got her, y'all," Dana told them, overcoming her fear of the evil fiend.

Melinda tossed a cobra at her and missed. Dana stomped its head and killed it. Then she kicked her head, knocking her to the ground. After that, she pulled a knife from her pocket and stabbed Melinda's heart. She screamed bloody murder as she died very painfully.

Melinda Kale went howling back to the endless fires of hell.

MIRANDA: THE FINAL CONFLICT

It was a week later on Christmas Eve 2005 when residents of Bethel's Hollow requested that the tree was chopped down at Witches' Gallows Lane after blaming it for many of the deaths that'd recently occurred. Several officers went down there. One sawed it down. Others poured gasoline on it and struck matches to it. The residents cheered as they watched it burn. The officers stayed after everyone left. They weren't happy for long. It was like a bomb going off in their faces when a boom knocked them down and set them on fire.

Then Miranda Kale-the youngest of the Kale Witches- rose from her grave. She was wearing a black robe. She had long, brown hair. She laughed at the officers' horrible pain. Then she took her machete and butchered them one by one.

"Not such a merry Christmas!" she snarled.

Seconds later, Kyle began having trouble sleeping. When he woke up and wiped his eyes, he saw Miranda at the foot of his bed.

"Holy shit!" he shrieked.

She stabbed him in his chest numerous times. Then he was dead. When his parents Herschel and Susan Wright ran into the room, they couldn't believe their eyes. Before Herschel could hold his rifle at Miranda, she drove her machete into his heart and said, "That's what I was doing in your house!"

Herschel fell to the floor and bled to death. She grabbed Susan after that and stabbed her in the back countless times until she was dead.

Hours later, Gilda woke up by hearing a knock on the door. She answered and saw Miranda standing there.

"Merry Christmas. How can I help you?"

"Not as merry as you think."

"What are you talking about?"

"Miranda Kale, the youngest of the Kale Witches, is risen from her grave. She's claimed ten lives so far. Herschel, Susan, and Kyle were three of them."

Miranda gave her a grin.

"Holy shit!" Gilda shrieked. "Get the hell outta my house right now, you damn demon!"

Miranda grabbed her jaws and stabbed her stomach numerous times until she died. Veronica was woken up by her daughter's eerie screams. But Miranda was gone before she could see her. She found Gilda's body in a puddle of blood and screamed bloody murder.

It was that evening when Father Kennedy had Christmas supper with Danielle's family.

After the meal, he called Dana and Danielle to have several words with him.

"Miranda Kale, the youngest of the Kale Witches, is risen from her grave. She's claimed twelve lives so far. Kyle and Gilda were two of them."

Tears streamed down the girls' faces.

"Say it's not true," Dana told him.

"I wish I could. The curse at Witches' Gallows Lane is alive as we speak. May the grace of our Lord Jesus Christ be with you."

He left with that.

At around one a.m., Dana woke Danielle up and said, "We gotta go!"

"Go where?"

"Witches' Gallows Lane!"

"You got it!"

When they got there, Father Kennedy was waiting in his brown station-wagon. He rolled his window down and said, "I knew you two were coming."

Then he held a silver pitcher out and said, "You will need this."

"What is it?" Danielle asked.

"It's holy water."

"Gee, thanks."

"You're mostly welcomed."

The girls got back into the car. Danielle drove down the lane until she was at the hill.

"Where is she?" Dana wondered.

"She'll come. Just be patient."

Danielle got out of the car and saw Dana sitting there.

"What the hell are you doing? Get out!"

"I heard that!" Miranda said from behind the girls.

They quickly turned around and saw her. She swung her machete. Dana quickly grabbed it.

She got her hand cut but didn't let it stop her.

"Give it up, girl. You haven't got it in you."

"I can bet you a permanent vacation to hell that I do!"

"Bring it, bitch!"

"It's on!"

Dana shoved the machete back and cut Miranda's forehead. She screamed bloody murder as she fell to the ground. Dana snatched it from and stabbed her heart as Danielle quickly poured holy water on her face.

"It burns! It burns!" Miranda wailed.

"The burning's only gonna get worse where you're going!" Dana told her.

After Miranda was completely done for, the two heard sirens from up the road.

"We better leave before something even worse happens," Danielle thought.

Danielle hanged herself in her dorm at Mississippi State University on the night of Saturday, September 30, 2006; the night that she and Walter would've married. She was eighteen. Dana died in a car accident in her hometown in Raven's Stone, Tennessee, on Halloween Night 2006. She was nineteen. Father Kennedy died in his sleep at around three a.m. on Christmas Day 2006. He was seventy-one.

THE DIABOLICAL
PLAYGROUND

Coincidences, in general, are great stumbling-blocks in
the way of that class of thinkers who have been educated
to know nothing of the theory of probabilities.
Edgar Allan Poe, "The Murders in the Rue Morgue"

"Goodnight, y'all," Daphne told her work friends at Gibson Valley
Steakhouse after clocking out at eleven pm. When she got to her car,
she heard the Beatles' "A Hard Day's Night" on the radio and thought
that it was a song that she could relate because she'd been working all
evening. After a while, she saw "Devil's Playground" Lane and dared
herself to take a shortcut home through there. The playground hadn't
been used in decades because of the dreadful coincidences for which it
was blamed. In the late 1800s, a cult went there and held Black Mass
under the direction of a priest by the name of Cain Peruzzi. When
they were caught by a witch hunt in 1901, Peruzzi and his followers
were burned alive and buried on the ground. Decades later, the City of
Gibson Valley decided to place a recreational park there. In July 1932,

a recently married couple had a picnic lunch at the playground. A year later, the young woman died from

Hansen's disease during her fifth month of pregnancy. Hours after her funeral, her husband went out to the playground and hanged himself from the monkey bars. A young mother took her three-year-old son to play there in February 1934. Months later, the child died from yellow fever. A month later, she committed suicide by gunshot to the head.

Daphne slowed her car down and stared at the playground rides for a moment. Then a huge, purple toad leaped onto her windshield. It had yellow spots along with rows of teeth like a shark and forked tongue like a snake. She screamed bloody murder as she stomped the gas. The toad flew off. When she got home, she dialed her boyfriend Ethan's cell-phone number and heard him answer the second ring.

"Hello."

"Ethan?"

"Hey, girl!"

"Ethan! You've no earthly idea!"

"What the hell you talking about?"

"I dared myself to go by 'Devil's Playground' Lane."

"No way!"

"I've never seen anything so scary in my life!"

"What did you see?"

"I stopped to look at the playground. Then this purple toad jumps on my windshield. It had teeth like a shark. And a tongue just like a snake. It was evil!"

"No way!"

"Man! I gotta tell Marty!"

"Ethan, no! Y'all stay away from there! I mean it!"

"Hey, babe. I gotta go!"

"Ethan, stay-"

Click

Daphne rolled her eyes and growled, yanking her long, blond hair.

Ethan dialed his best friend Marty's phone number and heard him answer the second ring.

"Hello."

"Marty! You won't believe this shit Daphne just called me up and said!"

"What's up?"

"She was on her way home from work. And she dared herself to go through 'Devil's Playground' Lane. Now, she says this purple toad with teeth like a shark and tongue like a snake attacked her!"

Marty laughed and thought, "No way!"

"She said it."

"I gotta go see this shit!"

"Good luck," Ethan sighed.

"I'm going right now."

Marty got into his truck and drove to the playground. After he got out, he looked around and stared at the swing set, then looked to the monkey bars. He thought very hard for several minutes. Then he climbed to the top of them and walked until he stumbled over a humongous cottonmouth. The snake hissed furiously at him and bit his left heel. He screamed bloody murder and fell off after losing balance.

It was Sunday morning when Ethan woke up, being concerned for his friend. He dialed Marty's cell phone but didn't get an answer. Then he remembered the conversation that he had with him only hours earlier. He got into his truck and drove to the playground. He didn't see Marty's corpse at first. Everything around him was dead silent. His heart skipped a beat when he saw Marty lying there and heard the hissing of the snake. He jumped into his truck and sped away. When he got back to his house, he dialed Daphne's number and became anxious for her to answer. When she answered the second ring, he told her, "Daphne! You've no idea!"

"What the hell are you talking about?"

"Marty went out to that playground last night!"

"What?"

"I just went out there and found him lying dead and a huge snake hissing at me! I'm telling you that place has a devil's curse on it!"

"I tried to warn you, myself. You wouldn't listen to me."

After Ethan got off the phone with Daphne, he dialed Gibson Valley Police and heard the receptionist answer the first ring.

"Good morning, Gibson Valley Police. This is Teresa. How may I help you?"

"Yes, ma'am. This is Ethan Woodard. I'm calling to file a report."

"Go ahead, Mr. Woodard."

"It was on 'Devil's Playground' Lane. My best friend dared himself to go out there last night. I just found him this morning. Bit to death by a snake!"

"Okay, Mr. Woodard. Is this the whole truth, so help you, God?"

"As God as my Witness."

"Okay. We'll have someone out there to investigate shortly."

"Thank you."

"You're welcomed. Have a nice day."

Three nights later, Marty's family and friends gathered at Lewis Mortuary and Funeral Home as they lined up to view his corpse in a black suit and black tie and lying in a black casket. Daphne and Ethan sat with Miranda, Marty's girlfriend, in the smoke room. Suddenly, they were interrupted when the Rev. Dewey Myers walked in and sighed, "Good evening, y'all."

"Good evening, Brother Dewey," Miranda told him.

"How ya doing? I'm Ethan Woodard."

"And I'm Daphne Thatcher."

"Nice to meet y'all."

The room got very quiet. Then the reverend said, "I'd like to ask y'all a personal question."

"What's that?" Daphne asked.

"Have you made Jesus the Lord in your life?"

"Why do you ask that?" Miranda wondered.

"Good question. The reason I'm asking is your boyfriend took a challenge by going where he went. Before he went, he knew what was gonna happen to him and what God had prepared for him. He knew the Lord Jesus Christ as his personal Savior and wasn't gonna die lost and burn for eternity in a devil's hell!"

"We gotta go," Daphne said, rolling her eyes.

"That's up to you, Ms. Thatcher. You ain't even promised two seconds from now. And if you die rejecting the Lord, He's gonna tell you to depart from Him for He never knew you. Then you will be condemned to burn for eternity in a Satan's hell!"

He held his copy of the Holy Bible up and swore, "The Book don't lie!"

The three walked away.

On his way home, Ethan was thumbed down by an old midget who stood at three feet tall and wore a black tuxedo and red bowtie. He had long, reddish brown hair and pointy ears that would remind anyone of a character from one of JRR Tolkien's works. His face was very wrinkled like a raisin. His chin would remind anyone of Jay Leno. He looked like he could play the evil, old man who'd pop up from the casket and laugh to cause the teen girls to scream bloody murder inside the Halloween funhouse. Ethan stopped and rolled his window down.

"Do you need a ride somewhere, sir?"

"That's so kind of you, young man."

The old midget climbed into the cab of the truck like a normal-heighten person would climb the rungs of a ladder. As he fastened his seatbelt, he told Ethan, "I need a ride to 'Devil's Playground' Lane."

"Are you sure about that?"

"I'm positive. And I'd like to ask you a personal question. That's the reason I want you to take me there."

"What is it you wanna ask me?"

"Have you accepted Jesus as your personal Lord and Savior?"

"I have. Thank you very much."

Then Ethan got to "Devil's Playground" Lane and let the midget out.

"My name is Isaac by the way. Isaac Peruzzi."

"Alright, Isaac. What do you wanna show me?"

"Follow me."

Isaac led Ethan behind the slide and watched him pick up a small ax.

"What the hell?" Ethan wondered.

"They're calling your name at the fiery gate right now, Ethan!" Isaac laughed.

He tripped Ethan, causing him to fall to the ground. Then he forced the blade of the ax into the back of his head. A Gibson Valley officer could hear him from down the road. He jumped into his patrol car and sped to the playground. He found Ethan's gruesomely mutilated corpse lying there and staggered back, then vomited.

Everyone was upset about Ethan and Marty the next morning.

"I'm gonna go out there and find that sick bastard this evening!" Miranda swore to Daphne.

"I don't think it'll be a good idea," she told her.

"Why's that? Two people have been murdered out there in less than a week!"

"Miranda, don't go! You'll be killed. You're my best friend!"

"I'm going, Daphne. You're not stopping me! No one is!"

It was that night when Miranda drove out to the playground. She heard Daphne calling her cell phone but ignored her call. She just stared around until she saw a three-foot tall monkeylike creature having blue fur and a long, speared tail. It had horns on its head like a bull. She saw it riding one of the swings and say, "Hello, Miranda!"

It sounded like Linda Blair as the devil-possessed girl in The Exorcist. Miranda squealed as it leaped from the swing. Then it bludgeoned her forehead with its horns. She was dead in a matter of seconds. She was found by the police hours later.

Hours after Miranda's body was laid to rest several days later, Daphne drove out to the playground. When she got out of her car, she stared around until she saw the ax learning against the slide. She quickly walked over to get it until Isaac jumped into her way.

"Just what do you think you're doing, young lady?" he asked.

"Outta my way, little man!"

She ran around him and dashed to the slide. She picked the ax up and turned to Isaac. He begged for his life as she held it up. Then she swung it and chopped his head off. She looked around for several seconds until she heard the snake slithering toward her. She bent down and chopped its head in half. Then she felt someone tapping her shoulders. She turned to see the abnormal creature standing there, prepared to horn her to death. She lifted the ax and chopped its head in half. After that, she thought, "My work here is finished."

As she was driving home, she thought to herself, "Satan is one mysterious son of a bitch!"

THE MYSTERY of GOBLIN HILL

Perry sat in the library during his lunch period and browsed through the shelf. Finally, he came across The Dunwich Horror and Others. He took it from the shelf and opened it to the page of contents and found out that there was one of Lovecraft's works that he'd heard of and found interesting in it. He checked it out at the counter and sat at a table.

After a while, Samantha walked into the library and saw him. She smiled and waved to him.

"Hey," he whispered to her.

She walked to the table where he was sitting and asked, "What are you reading?"

"This is Howard Phillips Lovecraft, a master of the modern horror-story."

"Interesting."

"So, you like that weird stuff, too, I guess."

"I love that stuff, Perry! So what is it by him you're reading?"

"It's a horror short-story entitled 'The Terrible Old Man.'"

"That does sound spooky."

"Yeah, it does. And it reminds me of a local legend here in Duckford."

"How does it go?"

"They said to have seen this very old-looking midget riding a unicycle around Hartsfield Road at night. No one knows who he is or where he came from. Legend has it that he lives underground at that hill in the back of what the cemetery on that road. It's also been accorded to legend if you see him out at night, never act scared. Or else, he will come after you."

"That is scary."

"And you like that weird stuff really?"

"Yes, I do! I love it!"

"I never knew we could be this much alike."

"I never knew it, either, Perry."

"So, what are you doing after the game tonight?"

"I don't know. What are you doing?"

"I think my best friend Kenny and I may go and watch the game tonight. It is home, isn't it?"

"Yes, it is."

"Sounds great."

"Hopefully, I'll see ya there."

"Okay."

"I'll see you later, Perry."

"Bye."

Perry went back to his reading after Samantha walked out of the library. After a while, the bell rang. He went through the hall and was on his way to his last class for the day.

"Perry!" Kenny blurted out.

He turned to see his best friend walking toward him and asked, "What's up, Ken?"

"Not much. Whatcha doing?"

"I'm walking to that music class. That no one takes serious!"

"Oh, yeah?"

"Hell yeah!"

"You going to the game tonight?"

"I'm planning on it."

"I'll come getcha if ya need me to."

"Sounds great."

"I hope we win tonight."

"Me, too," Perry sighed.

Then Kenny recognized the book that Perry was carrying.

"Who's that book by?"

"That's HP Lovecraft."

"Who?"

"He's the most influential practitioner of the modern horror-story."

"Awesome."

"I didn't know you like to read, Kenny."

"Oh, yeah. I do."

"You do know that it's Halloween time, right?"

"Right."

"I was planning to do something tonight after the game."

"What's that?"

"I was wanting to go to that cemetery they call 'Goblin Hill.'"

"No way, man!"

"I was wanting to check that legend out."

"What legend?"

"About the midget who rides the unicycle around there at night. No one knows who he is. Legend has it that he dwells underground at that hill in the back of that cemetery. It's also been said that if you act scared when you see him, he'll come after you."

"I think they're full of horseshit to their eyebrows."

"There's only one way to find out."

It was that evening when they decided to not go to the football game but go watch a movie at the local theater instead. It was Kenny, his girlfriend Jennifer, and Perry. After the movie, they rode in Jennifer's car to Goblin Hill Cemetery. The three teens got out of the car and walked through the silver gate. As they walked around, it was dead silent all around except for the barking dogs at the residences on Hartsfield Road. They walked alongside the gravestones as Perry read dates of death on them early as 1857. Then they finally got to the hill and saw a small, wooden door.

"I dare you to open it!" Kenny told Perry with a laugh.

"Okay," he told him reluctantly.

His wrist trembled as he pulled the rusty knob. Then he opened the door and saw nothing inside except a brick wall covered in cobwebs. After that, he slammed the door shut and told Kenny and Jennifer, "We better get the hell outta here!"

"Good idea," Jennifer said, getting nervous.

They were on their way back to the car. Suddenly, a small man who stood at three feet tall rode in on a red unicycle as he wore a black hat like the Witch of the West, a red, collared shirt, and dark-brown slacks along with black, pointy shoes. He had long, white, stringy hair as his face was very wrinkled. He raised a silver sickle to a tire in the back of Jennifer's car and slashed it.

"Oh, my God! Look what he did to my car!"

Jennifer was crushed as she burst into tears. The goblin pulled his hat off and yelled a word in an unknown language. Then a golden toad leaped from his hat and exhaled fire at them. The fire circled around them as the midget rode his unicycle over it and rode off. When the fire quickly died down, the toad spoke.

"His name is Ferdinand. And he lives underground at that hill in that cemetery. At night, he rides these roads alone. If you see him, don't act afraid. Or else, you will die!"

Then the toad did a front flip into the air and never came back down.

"I gotta call for help!" Jennifer thought.

She quickly got her cell phone out and tried to dial her mom's number. On the second ring, she heard her mom answer by saying, "Hello."

"Mom?"

"Jennifer?"

"Yeah, it's me! Perry, Kenny, and I are out here at that cemetery that they call Goblin Hill Cemetery."

"Uh-huh."

After that, Kenny and Perry watched Ferdinand ride up behind her, holding his sickle up.

"Jennifer! Watch out!" Perry screamed.

She quickly turned around and saw him swing the sickle and slash her chests. She screamed an eerie scream as she fell to the ground.

"Jennifer!" Kenny screamed.

He ran to her and saw that she was bleeding heavily. Then he thought, "I gotta call nine-one-one!"

Perry got his cell phone out and dialed the number.

"9-1-1. What's the emergency?"

"Yes, I need an ambulance for-"

The phone went dead.

Then the boys heard police sirens coming down the road. An officer got out of his car and asked, "What seems to be the problem, gentlemen?"

Kenny's face was red and soaked in tears as Perry answered, "Officer, there's been a murder, here. It was a midget riding a unicycle like a clown in a circus. As God as my Witness! No lie!"

"I swear, I'm gonna start charging everyone a quarter for telling me bullshit bout some murderous goblin who roams this cemetery and this road at night. I'll probably be able to retire early as next Christmas."

"You gotta believe us, Officer!" Kenny told him. "He just swore to God!"

"Y'all, get your ass down on that ground and not another damn word till I tell you otherwise!" the officer screamed.

Kenny and Perry got onto the ground as two other officers approached them. They searched them and handcuffed them. After they put them in the back of a police car, the officers searched Jennifer's car. Then they took them to the station and contacted their parents. Perry's dad picked them up and took Kenny home.

"What were y'all doing at that cemetery, Perry? Were y'all drinking? Were y'all doing drugs?"

Perry didn't answer. He just sat there until his dad raised his voice in anger.

"Answer me! Dammit!"

"Dad, one of my best friends was just murdered! So, just give me some space. Please!"

"You better watch yourself."

The officers awaited the paramedics to come and haul Jennifer's corpse to the autopsy room at Duckford Memorial Hospital. The one, who ordered Kenny and Perry to surrender, lit a cigarette and told one of his buddies, "I told them kids I'm gonna start charging a quarter to everyone who gives me bullshit bout some bloodthirsty goblin riding these roads at night."

He sucked on his cigarette again and turned his head to see Ferdinand riding toward the cemetery.

"Hey! Look that way!"

He pointed toward the gate. The older officer looked and saw Ferdinand riding through.

"Holy shit!" he thought as he saw him swinging the sickle.

Ferdinand began pedaling faster and got behind the younger officer, then stabbed the back of his neck.

He coughed blood and fell to the ground. The other officer jumped back in unspeakable fright. He got on his walkie-talkie and shouted, "I need help down here!"

Ferdinand got off the unicycle and jumped down to the officer who was lying on the ground and in pain, then began stabbing his chests with the sickle. The other officer kept screaming through his walkie-talkie that he needed someone sent out there immediately. Then he sighed, "Too late."

"What the hell ya mean too late?" the officer demanded from the other line.

"This damn midget's already murdered McCann!"

"What midget?"

"That goblin that's believed to haunt this cemetery! He was riding a red unicycle when he came up and attacked McCann with a damn sickle."

"I think you're full of horseshit, Pickford."

"Well, you're more than welcomed to come out here and see for yourself if you'd like to."

"We'll send someone to be out there as soon as possible."

"Thanks!"

Then the paramedics arrived in the ambulance to take Jennifer's corpse to the autopsy room.

"Thank God that y'all are here!" Pickford yelled as he was out of breath. "What the hell took y'all so damn long?"

"We've no time to explain," one paramedic answered as he and the other one picked Jennifer's corpse up.

Then they recognized McCann's corpse lying on the ground and Ferdinand's sickle lying next to it.

"What the hell?" the paramedic wondered.

He and his co-worker looked up at Pickford as he guessed, "So, you're the killer after all Pickford."

"Holy shit! Don't you even dare!"

Pickford pulled his pistol out at the paramedics and said, "Don't you dare come near me! Neither wanna y'all!"

After that, sirens were heard as a police car drove down the road.

"Paul Pickford, put the gun down immediately!" the officer ordered through the megaphone.

Pickford shot at the windshield and shattered it with the bullet.

"That's it!" the officer said with his teeth grinded.

He jumped out and walked slowly around Pickford, then put his pistol to the side of his head.

"Put the gun down, Pickford!"

Pickford was shaking as he dropped his pistol. Then the officer handcuffed him and said, "You have the right to remain silent; anything you say can and will be used against you in a court of law. You have the right to an attorney. If you cannot afford an attorney, one will be appointed for you. Do you understand these rights?"

Pickford turned his head and spat in the officer's face. Then he hissed, "This man's calling me a murderer!"

"Mr. Pickford, I'm gonna ask you to calm down."

"It was the damn midget! I saw him! Dammit!"

One of the paramedics handed over the sickle that had a blade soaked in blood.

"I swear! I'm not the killer!"

"You're gonna have to take that up with the judge," the officer insisted.

In the Sunday newspaper, Kenny was reading about Officer Paul Pickford's arrest and that he would serve life or the death penalty if convicted for the murder of Officer Richard "Ricky" McCann. After he read the article, Kenny dialed Perry's number. He answered the second ring.

"Hello!"

"Perry?"

"What's up, Kenny?"

"Did you read the paper today?"

"No. What happened?"

"They think that older cop, you know Pickford?"

"Yeah."

"They think he murdered Jennifer."

"What the hell?"

"He swore that he and Ricky McCann were out there, waiting for the ambulance to take her to the autopsy room when the midget Ferdinand came riding on his unicycle and butchered McCann with a sickle. He got on his walkie-talkie and ranted bout the midget killing him. The officer from the other line wouldn't believe him. Then the paramedics arrived to pick Jennifer's body up. That was when they discovered a sickle covered in blood lying next to McCann's body."

"So, that's why they think Pickford did it?"

"That's what they said in the newspaper."

"So, they arrested him?"

"Yeah, Reid did. Reid said when he arrived, Pickford was aiming his pistol at the paramedics. When he ordered him to put it down, he shot Reid's windshield out."

"That's crazy!"

"Yeah, it's crazy."

"I wonder how they're gonna find out he's innocent."

"Who knows?"

It was around midnight when Pickford lied sound asleep on his cot at the town lockup. Then he was woke up by Ferdinand saying, "Oh, Paulie."

He quickly woke up and jumped from where he was sleeping.

"Who the hell are you?"

"You've forgotten me already?"

"I don't wanna remember. That's probably why."

"I'm the real one who really killed Jennifer Islander and Ricky McCann."

"Please, leave! Now!"

"First of all, Paul, I'd like to give you something that you desperately want."

"You don't know what I want! You don't know me!"

"I know you don't wanna serve life in prison for a crime that you're innocent of; I know that much."

"No! I don't!"

"Then come closer."

"Alright."

When he got closer, Ferdinand violently forced the sickle into Pickford's eye and plucked it out. He grunted in pain. After that, Ferdinand cut deeper into his face and took pleasure of his pain. He was gone before the officers on graveyard shift could see him.

Kenny picked Perry up for school hours later. On the local radio station, they heard the morning-show host announce, "We just got word that former Duckford policeman Paul Henry Pickford was found dead in his cell at the town jail early this morning. They suspect he was murdered but they don't know who it could've been. Officer Eric Reid said that the sickle that Pickford was said to have used to commit the murders of 17-year-old Jennifer Islander and 27-year-old Duckford policeman Richard "Ricky" McCann was missing."

Kenny changed the station to another station and heard the morning-show host announcing, "63-year-old Paul Henry Pickford, a former Duckford policeman, was found dead in his cell at the city jail this morning at around midnight."

He changed the station and heard the same thing. Suddenly, he drove into the students' parking lot at Duckford High School and parked it in his place. When he and Perry got into the courtyard, Samantha ran up to them and said, "Kenny! Perry! Oh, my God!"

She embraced Kenny and Perry tightly and let tears run from her brown eyes.

"I'm so sorry," she sobbed.

"I know," Kenny whispered. "She's in a much better place."

"That's all we can hope for."

The three were very quiet throughout the day until they were signed out to prepare for Jennifer's funeral that was at two o'clock. After the minister finished talking at the black casket in which her corpse was laid, he said a prayer and everyone left the graveyard.

It was that night when Kenny went outside and lit a cigarette on his front porch. Then he heard his cell phone ring. On the caller ID, he read RESTRICTED. He reluctantly answered by saying, "Hello."

"Hi, Kenny."

"Who's this?"

"You don't remember me?"

"Actually, I don't."

"We met at the cemetery the other night."

"I think you're doing drugs, you sick mother-"

42

The person hung up from the other line. Then Ferdinand wheeled around the corner, riding his unicycle, and demanded, "I'm doing a whole lot more well than you're about to be!"

"Holy shit!" Kenny shrieked.

He thought to himself, "I gotta get my gun!"

He ran upstairs to his bedroom and grabbed his pistol. When he came back, he saw that Ferdinand was gone.

"Better run!"

Ferdinand was riding down the road until he saw Samantha driving her car on the way home from working at the local grocery-store. She slammed on the brake as he got in his way and blew the horn. He stuck his thumb up and pedaled toward her. She rolled her window down and asked, "May I help you?"

"So, Sammy. You say you like that spooky stuff, don't you?"

"How do you know me?"

"I know everything."

"I gotta go. You're freaking me out, little man."

She rolled her window up and drove away. Ferdinand quickly pedaled behind her as she saw him in her rearview mirror.

"I better call the police."

She got her cell phone out. Before she could press the second digit, she heard Ferdinand shatter the back window with his sickle. She squealed as she quickly pulled her car to the side. She got out and looked angrily at the grotesque and small man.

"Have you lost your damn mind?" she screamed.

"I've lost my mind a long time ago, missy!" he laughed.

He eagerly jumped onto her back and grabbed her in a chokehold. She began punching and kicking as she fought for air. Then he quickly stabbed her heart countless times and laughed as she heavily bled. He let her fall to the damp ground. She died in a puddle of blood then and there.

Minutes later, Officer Eric Reid drove by on his way to work and recognized the shattered back window on her car and her driver's door widely opened with blood on it and the window.

"Holy Jesus Christ!" he thought.

He got on his walkie-talkie and said, "This is Officer Sergeant Eric Reid."

"Go ahead."

"I was driving on my way to work. Now, I'm on Root Road and I see that a murder's taken place just minutes ago. I happen to find a white Sedan with a broke-out window in the back. The driver's door's wide open with blood all over. And I've found the victim to be a white female about seventeen or eighteen years old. Long, black hair. Five feet and eight inches tall."

He looked through her purple purse and found her Mississippi driver's license and said, "I found her identity on a Mississippi driver's license. She was Samantha Ann Richton. Her date of birth was April 22, 1988. That means she had to have been sixteen. Her weight was estimated at around one-thirty."

The other officer contacted her parents. It had them crushed and in tears.

At school the next morning, everyone was upset after they got the news about Samantha's death, especially Perry.

"It'll be okay, man," Kenny told him. "She's in a much better place."

Perry continued to cover his face with his hands and sob.

"Ferdinand is going down!" he said after he uncovered his face and grinded his teeth.

It was around eleven o'clock that night when Perry called Kenny and heard him answer the second ring.

"Hello."

"Kenny?"

"What's up, Perry?"

"Are you ready?"

"Ready for what?"

"To go out there."

"Out where?"

"The cemetery."

"What cemetery?"

"For Christ sake, Goblin Hill!"

"Oh, yeah!"

"So, let's go!"

"Okay," Kenny sighed.

Minutes later, Kenny drove up. When Perry got into his car, he hauled ass to Hartsfield Road. He drove down the road until Ferdinand jumped in front of him with his unicycle. Kenny slammed on the brake and put the car into park.

"You're going down, little man!" Kenny told him as he slammed the car door and ran toward him.

"Catch me if you can!" Ferdinand laughed.

He pedaled toward the cemetery and pulled something from his pocket. The boys couldn't believe what it was: a human skull! Ferdinand threw it like a pitcher throwing the baseball to the batter during the World Series. It hit Perry in his face and shattered into pieces. There were chunks of brain all over him.

"God, this is gross!" he thought.

Kenny took his pistol out and fired it at Ferdinand, who was pedaling his unicycle toward the hill at the cemetery. He was frustrated that he missed and snapped, "Dammit!"

"I'm gonna get him!"

Perry followed Kenny into the cemetery as he ran in, continuing to fire his pistol. Ferdinand rode his unicycle down into his lair in the hill.

"You can run, but you damn sure can't hide!" Kenny swore.

Kenny fired his pistol again even though it was pitch black inside Ferdinand's lair. A second later, he and Perry heard him wail in horrible pain.

"I think I got him," Kenny said.

"Awesome."

Kenny struck his cigarette-lighter and walked forward, then saw Ferdinand lying on the ground and his unicycle gone.

"Rest in hell, Ferdinand!" Kenny snarled, aiming the pistol at his face.

Then he pulled the trigger and let the pistol fire. After that, he dialed the Duckford Police and heard an answer on the second ring.

"Yes, ma'am, this is Kenny Kingston. I'm calling about information on the murders that'd recently occurred here round town."

"Go ahead."

"Well, I just caught the murderer here at Goblin Hill Cemetery."

"Hold, please."

Several seconds later, Kenny had a policeman on the other line.

"Good evening, Officer."

"Good evening to you, too, Mr. Kingston. How may I help you?"

"Well, y'all are aware of the fact that Officer Paul Pickford, who's no longer with us, didn't murder my girlfriend Jennifer Islander or that cop Ricky McCann, right?"

"I guess you could say that."

"Well, I know who the real murderer is. He attacked my best friend and me on Hartsfield Road just a while ago. And I shot him to death. We have his body with us. We just need someone to come and pick it up."

"You got it. I'll have someone out there with you boys shortly."

"Thank you."

"You're most welcomed. Goodnight."

Kenny hung up and told Perry, "The cops are on their way."

"Great! Do we get a reward?"

After a while, two policemen rode up to the cemetery. Kenny and Perry walked aboveground as they carried Ferdinand's corpse.

"Thank you, gentlemen," Reid told them.

"It was a lotta work," Perry sighed.

"But I bet it's worth it."

"Worth what?"

"Go see the judge at the city court in the morning for your reward."

"How much?"

"Five grand."

"What?" Perry wondered.

"You know we're gonna split that, right?" Kenny declared.

"Oh, yeah of course."

"Well, once again, Reid sighed, thanks, boys. And y'all have a good night."

After a while, Perry was asleep in his bed until his cell phone rang. He didn't recognize the number. He answered anyway and said, "Hello."

"Hi, Perry."

"Who's this?"

"You'll find soon enough, I promise that."

"Okay."

"I hear you're getting a reward."

"Yeah, I am. I'm excited."

"Don't get too excited."

"Don't get too excited?"

"What makes you think you're gonna live to spend it?"

THE GARDEN OF HADES

Brandy was driving on her way home from her boyfriend Mike's house one cool night in December night in 2006. When she got near the cemetery, she saw a red beam of light come from the gate. She got closer and saw it disappear. She thought that it'd came from the cave behind the cemetery. Legend had it that the cave led the way to hell. During the spring, the bushes in the cemetery were covered in red roses. Those were the two reasons that the people of Bethel's Hollow, Mississippi, nicknamed the place "Garden of Hades" Cemetery.

She stared for a moment, then drove off. She got on the phone with her best friend Stacy and heard her answer the second ring.

"Hello."

"Stacy! You won't believe this!"

"What's up, girl?"

"I was just passing the cemetery."

"The one they call 'Garden of Hades?'"

"Yeah. And there was a beam of light that shot out from that cave! You would not believe it!"

"You know the legend about that cemetery, don't you?"

"They say that cave leads to hell."

"That legend's probably true."

"I gotta go check that out."

"I'd rather that you didn't, Stacy."

"I'm going to check it out. I'll talk to you later, Brandy."

"Bye," Brandy sighed and hung up.

Stacy dialed her friend Anthony and heard him answer the second ring.

"Hello."

"What's going on, Anthony?"

"You'll never believe what Brandy just called me and said."

"She and Mike are getting married?"

"Not even close!"

"What did she say?"

"It was about that cemetery they call 'Garden of Hades.'"

"I've heard the legend about that place. I think it's a joke."

"You don't believe there's a hell?"

"I told you that I'm agnostic. I don't think heaven or hell can be proven. I don't believe in Allah, Jehovah, or any of that other bullshit."

"But would you like to go out there with me tonight?"

"Sure," he sighed.

"I'll come over there and pick you up."

"Cool."

"See you in a few minutes."

Several minutes later, Stacy drove into Anthony's driveway. He went out there and got into her car. She drove to the cemetery. When they got there, it was very peaceful and dead silent. They looked to the cave and watched it light up. They walked close to it. A minute later, they heard sounds that sounded like tormented souls. Stacy became uncomfortable.

"Anthony," she said.

"What's going on?"

"That's really scaring me."

Suddenly, a black hearse drove out of the cave at ninety miles per hour and chased the two toward the gate. They were running for their lives. It ran over Stacy and knocked her down. After that, it ran over her, crushing her skull. Anthony was running for his house until a black Volkswagen stopped for him.

"Would you like a ride?" the elderly woman, who was driving the car, asked him.

"I would love that! Thank you very much, ma'am."

He got in and closed the door.

"What's your name, kid?" she asked him.

"Anthony Harvey."

"I'm Delilah Beard."

"This is very kind of you, Mrs. Beard."

"Please! Call me Delilah!"

"I think that'd be impolite, ma'am."

"I insist."

"Whatever makes you comfortable, ma'am."

She put her foot on the gas and asked him, "Now, Anthony, what are your religious beliefs?"

"I'm an agnostic."

"Oh, really. You believe that the Lord's existence is not provable."

"That's what I believe. I'm not saying for sure that I believe that He doesn't exist. I read Darwin's observation On the Origin of Species. He admitted that he could've been incorrect. There had to be a Creator responsible for it. I believe I'll meet Him someday. I don't believe in Him as Allah, Jehovah, or any of that bullshit."

"You know, Darwin was agnostic, himself."

"So was HL Mencken, another philosopher who favored Darwin. Nietzsche and Ayn Rand were atheists. Freud was an atheist."

"By the way, where are you headed?"

"I'm headed home. I'll give you directions."

When he got home, he dialed the police and reported, "This is Anthony Harvey. I'm calling to file a report on an incident at 'Garden of Hades' Cemetery. My friend Stacy Kane and I went out there just tonight when a black hearse came zooming outta that cave and ran over her and killed her. I didn't see the driver at all."

"Do you promise?" the officer asked.

"So help me, God."

"We'll have some officers go out there to investigate. I'll tell you, I've been with the police for twelve years. And tonight, if someone could pay me a dollar for every tall-tale for people seeing a bloodthirsty demon out at that cemetery, I'd retire tomorrow."

"I understand."

"Have a good night."

It was hours after Stacy's funeral when Anthony was listening to Kenny Chesney's "Who You'd Be Today" on a local radio-station. Finally, he turned the station, having tears in his hazel eyes because it was the song that was played for her. After that, his cell phone rang. He answered it by saying, "Hello."

"Hi, Anthony."

"Who's this?"

"This is Delilah."

"How do you know my number?"

"I'll consider that my own business."

"How may I help you, Delilah?"

"I'd like to show you something."

"What's that?"

"I'll be there shortly. Wait for me."

"Okay."

He stood out there and waited until she drove up. He got into her car. When she drove to the cemetery, he said, "Please, Delilah! No!"

"You're gonna feel so much better when you see your surprise. I guarantee it."

He walked with her until she stopped at a gravestone. She flashed a cigarette lighter on it. He read on it:

ANTHONY ANDREW HARVEY

APR 18 1987

DEC 10 2006

"Holy shit!" he shrieked, backing away.

He looked at her and snarled, "You are one sick bitch!"

She drew a machete from behind herself and scared him shitless. She chopped his right arm off and cackled as he screamed bloody murder. He bled heavily as he fell to the ground, kicking and screaming. She chopped his left arm and laughed as he continued to bleed. After that, she chopped both of his legs off. He was now barely alive. She kicked his face and said, "You say you're not sure of the Creator that you believe in, Anthony?"

"Oh, God! Please help me!"

Anthony was helpless as he lied there armless and legless until Delilah chopped his head off and snarled, "Rest in pieces, bitch!"

She shoved his body parts into the pit.

For several days, Anthony was missing. No one knew what had happened to him. Mike dared himself to go out to the cemetery. Then he discovered the pit and couldn't believe what he saw! Then he saw a winged creature having the body of a hyena with red fur, black spots, and speared tail fly up.

"What the hell?" he wondered.

The hellhound exhaled fire onto Mike and picked him up with his claws. It carried him into the cave. It was the next morning when Brandy found a folded-up sheet of white paper on her pillow and opened it up. She read it to herself.

Dear Brandy,

If you're reading this, Mike and Anthony have already made it to where they were going. But don't worry. My faithful servants are taking good care of them. If you want to know who's writing, we can meet at my place behind the cemetery @ sundown.

"I'm gonna get that sick bastard!" she thought.

Hours later, she drove to the cemetery and saw Delilah standing there. She was grinning as she said, "Hello, Brandy."

"I know what you're up to."

Delilah drew the machete. Brandy snatched it by the handle and got it from the old woman.

"Who's the bitch now?"

She stabbed Delilah's heart and listened as she screamed bloody murder, falling to the ground. After that, the hearse drove out of the cave along with the hellhound. The hellhound exhaled fire at her. She dodged and watched it get onto the hearse. It exploded onto the fiendish creature, burning it to death. Brandy jumped into her car and sped away like a bat out of hell.

THE NIGHTMARE OVER
RAVEN'S STONE

Dreams are often most profound when they seem the most crazy.
Sigmund Freud

It was the summer of 1989 when five-year-old Ryan Gautier finally fell asleep at midnight. He was afraid to because of Simon, the evil goblin that'd been terrorizing his dreams for the past month. An hour after he fell asleep, Ryan had a dream. He saw himself in his mid teens and with a blond girl who was in her mid teens as well. Simon was with them inside a vacant house when Ryan looked him in his eyes and said, "I believe in Jesus. I believe in Santa Claus. I believe in the Easter Bunny. I believe in the Tooth Fairy, even. But you, Simon. You're a phony."

Simon began shaking in fear as he watched Ryan take out a bottle of kerosene and a box of matches.

"Don't do that! Please!" he begged.

Ryan tossed kerosene on Simon and struck a match. He tossed it onto him. He and the girl laughed as they watched Simon catch on fire. After that, Ryan woke up from the dream and ran to his parents Jean-Claude and Marie's bedroom, shouting, "Daddy! Mommy!"

"Son, it's one in the morning," Jean-Claude mumbled.

"I did it!"

"Did what?" Marie asked.

"I killed him!"

"Killed who?" Jean-Claude asked.

"Simon! That bad elf who was in my dreams!"

"You got him?" Marie guessed as she rose from her side of the bed.

"Yeah! I got him!"

"That's great! Now, you go on back to bed. Simon's dead now. He can't bother you anymore. Okay?"

"Okay, Mommy."

Ryan ran back to his room and went back to sleep.

TEN YEARS LATER

Ryan grew up as a US Navy brat because of his father. In autumn 1999, Jean-Claude was stationed in Tennessee and bought the family a house in Raven's Stone, which was near Pigeon Forge. It was a late-October day when he and Ryan walked into the counselor's office at Raven's Stone High School. She smiled and said, "You must be Ryan Gautier."

"Yes, ma'am."

"I've been expecting you."

She went over his schedule with him and gave it to him, then sent him on his way.

"Have a great day, y'all," she told them.

"You do the same, Mrs. Paulsen."

He walked down the hall and saw a beautiful, young woman. He couldn't believe who she was! She was the same girl in his dream!

"Hi," she told him.

"Hi," he told her. "I'm Ryan Gautier, the new boy."

"Kate McHenry."

"Where you from, Ryan?"

"Mississippi."

"What part?"

"Duckford."

"I've never heard of that place."

"It's a small town most people never heard of."

"Like Raven's Stone."

Then Mr. Bob Root, the high-school assistant principal, walked out of the faculty lounge and saw them.

"Ms. McHenry!" he snapped.

"Yes, sir," she answered.

"Where are you supposed to be at this time?"

She looked to Ryan and said, "Bye, Ryan!"

"Bye, Kate."

Ryan walked into one classroom and asked, "Is this Ms. Gilberts's class?"

"That's me. What do you want?"

"I'm Ryan Gautier, your new student."

"Well, just take a seat. Any seat that's not taken."

Ryan walked down one aisle and sat behind a boy who was asleep. All of a sudden, Ms. Gilberts recognized him sleeping and snapped, "Mr. Maker!"

He woke up and screamed, "Let it go, Simon! It's over!"

Ms. Gilberts was concerned for his behavior as he was punching himself in the jaw and asked, "Brett, would you like to share with the class what that was about?"

"NO!" he shouted as he stood up.

"Maybe Mr. Root would like to. Go! Now!"

"You got it, sister!"

Brett slammed the door as he walked into the hall.

In the boys' restroom, he stared into the mirror and said, "He's only a dream, Brett. He can't hurt you. He doesn't even exist for Christ sake!"

Suddenly, Simon appeared behind his shoulder like Bloody Mary would according to that urban legend. Brett quickly turned around and felt the evil fiend claw his eyes. He was screaming bloody murder as he fell into the floor. Mr. Root ran into the restroom and saw that Simon and the blood from Brett's eyeballs were gone.

"Brett Maker, have you gone simply mad?"

"It's not what you think, Mr. Root. I was really attacked!"

He snatched Brett from the floor and snarled with his teeth grinded.

"What the hell do you think you're doing? Does your mother know you smoke crack?"

"What? I don't even smoke cigarettes."

"Do you have any idea how many nasty diseases you can get from rolling around in a public restroom? You just made me waste a lot of my time for you. Do you know what the penalty you'll suffer for that?"

"Suspension?"

"You guessed it!"

Brett shrugged his shoulders and said, "Like I care."

"Get to class! You've got me upset enough at you already!"

After Ms. Gilberts's class ended, Brett and Ryan walked together. Brett began telling him about seeing Simon in his dream.

"Did he look like one of Santa's elves that woke up from sleeping overnight in a crypt?" Ryan asked.

"How would that look?"

"Ever heard the legend about sleeping overnight inside a crypt? You wake up with snow-white hair and you're crazy like a fox."

"Oh, yeah! That's interesting!"

"What did the principal give you for that incident?"

"He suspended me for a day."

"Where are you going now?"

"I have band."

"I guess I'll see you around."

"Bye, Ryan."

Then Kate came up to him and asked, "Who do you have next?"

"Mrs. Barman for world literature."

"Oh! So do I! We can walk together."

"That'll be good."

When they walked into the classroom, Mrs. Barman asked Ryan, "Who are you?"

"I'm Ryan Gautier, your new student."

"Okay. Just take any seat that's not taken."

"You can sit next to me," Kate whispered.

"I like that shirt," she whispered to him as she recognized Paul McCartney on his shirt of the Beatles.

"Thanks," he whispered back to her.

At the end of the period, he and Kate walked toward the cafeteria for lunch.

"What's their food like?" he asked her.

"Today, their having spaghetti. It's terrible."

"Well, I guess I'll stay in the library."

"Okay. I'll stay with you. I guess you like reading, too."

"I like to read."

Ryan looked around in the library and found a nonfiction book that he thought to be interesting: The Interpretation of Dreams by Sigmund Freud. He took it to the counter where Mr. Stanley, the middle-aged librarian, was sitting.

"Whatcha got there?" he asked.

"It's a book by Freud," Ryan answered.

"I see you're a fan of psychology."

"I guess you could say that. I think Freud had some quite interesting ideas."

"He did. I agree with you on that."

"Actually, I read the title of this book and thought about what Joseph in the Bible and how he could interpret dreams. I had these nightmares when I was a little kid. And sometimes, I wonder what he would've told me."

"I wouldn't wanna know," Mr. Stanley thought.

"Sometimes, I say the same."

"Well, it's very nice to meet you-"

"I'm Ryan Gautier. I just got here today."

"Well, I'm Mr. Lionel Stanley. I'm the librarian."

After lunch, Ryan and Kate walked down the hall together and saw Brett with his cousin Marvin Maker, who was a high-school senior.

"Hi, guys," Brett told them.

"Hi, Brett," Kate told him. "How are you?"

"I'm doing good. Marvin, this is Ryan, the new boy."

"Marvin Maker," he said, shaking hands with Ryan.

"Marvin, Ryan knows about Simon."

"Simon who?"

"Simon! The goblin who's been terrorizing our dreams the past several nights."

Marvin had no clue what his cousin was talking about. Kate looked at her watch and said, "I gotta get to my class, y'all. I'll see y'all later."

"Bye, Kate," Brett told her.

She walked away.

"Hey, y'all. Do you know where Coach Doug McGee's PE class is?" Ryan asked the Maker boys.

"I have him this period. You can walk with me."

In the gym, Ryan walked up to Coach McGee and told him, "I'm Ryan Gautier, your new student."

"It's very nice to meet you."

"You, too."

For the assignment, Coach McGee had the boys play badminton. During the last fifteen minutes, he told them, "Hit the showers."

Brett was soaping down in the shower when he saw fingernails that looked anything but human force their way up the drain. They poked the bottom of his feet and caused them to bleed. He ran into the locker room, screaming bloody murder.

"Hey! He's outta the closet! Irving McCool laughed.

"Shut up, McFool!" Brett shouted.

Irving jerked him by his throat and snapped, "What the hell did I tell you bout calling me that?"

"I think you are a fool," Ryan told him.

"What the hell did you just call me, new boy?"

"You heard me, McFool."

All the boys were laughing for Ryan. Irving didn't think that he was so tough when he opened his locker and saw Simon there. Simon began his eerie laugh as Irving slammed his locker. He was frightened to tears.

"Ha! McFool, the crybaby!" Brett laughed.

All the other boys began laughing at the most-respected member of the Raven's Stone Lions' football team. The laughter drifted into Coach McGee's office. He stormed into the locker room.

"For Christ sake, I thought there was a wild pack o' hyenas on the loose in here! What the hell's going on?"

Irving's best friend Albert Cook covered his face as he tried to laugh.

"Irving just got told off by the gaywot!"

"What gaywot?"

Brett had his Tasmanian Devil boxer-shorts on as he ran and kicked Albert's chests.

"You little!" Albert swore.

He punched Brett's chest and shouted, "That hurt!"

"You hurt my feelings. What's wrong with me hurting yours?"

"That's it!" Albert swore as he swung at Brett.

Ryan ran and body-slammed Albert onto the bench, causing it to break.

"Gautier! That'll get you suspended!" Coach McGee told him.

After that, the room was loud until Craig, the security guard, walked in and yelled, "Knock it off!"

The room was dead silent after that.

"Now, the people to start this, step forth! Now!"

Ryan and Brett took the blame.

"What happened, Brett?" Craig asked.

"Actually, it's a long story because y'all will all think I'm psycho if I tell you the real reason my foot began bleeding in the shower. That was when I ran out into the locker room, naked like a jaybird and screaming like an idiot. Then McFool started that about me coming outta the closet."

"Well, are you like that?"

"No, I am not. Mind your own business."

Then Craig said, "Brett and the new boy, y'all follow me. And y'all all go on back to your business."

The next day was Wednesday, October 20, 1999. Brett was typing on his computer in his bedroom that afternoon. He had thought up a poem for Kate. The poem talked of her long, blond hair and gorgeously blue eyes. Suddenly, a red mole having green spots on its back jumped through the screen, shattering it.

"What the hell?" Brett shrieked as he jumped from the computer.

Then he saw Simon standing there, laughing.

"Go to hell, Simon!" Brett growled.

"What's going on?" Leslie, Brett's mom, wondered when she walked into the room.

She couldn't believe what she was seeing when she saw Simon standing there winding up something that looked to be a Jack-in-the-box. It made a musical sound until an electric eel popped out and landed on her, electrocuting her. She fell to the floor and died. Simon burst into laughter as Brett blurted out, "You killed my mother, you bastard!"

He ran down the street to Marvin's house and banged on the door.

"What the hell you want, Brett?" Marvin snapped, swinging the door opened.

He was very teary-eyed when he said, "My mom was just killed."

"How?"

"Simon! He's not just a dream anymore!"

The Raven's Stone Police were investigating Leslie's death at her house. They pronounced her Dead at the Scene. They took her body to the hospital for an autopsy report. Hours later, Brett received a call.

"Hi, this is Dr. Mitchell. I did the autopsy work on Ms. Leslie Maker."

"Yes."

"Well, we found it true that her death was truly homicide. She was electrocuted."

"No shit!"

"I see. You and your mother were burglarized. Fortunate for you, you escaped the murderer. Unfortunate for your mother, she didn't."

"The murderer isn't even human to be honest."

"Well, we couldn't prove that."

"I don't know what to say."

"I'm sorry for your loss, kid. Hopefully, things will get better."

"Thanks," Brett told him and hung up.

It was the next evening when Ryan was enjoying the autumn weather as he was raking the section of dead leaves up and putting them into a wheelbarrow to haul. As soon as he got a full load, he hauled it to an abandoned cemetery that was down the road. He walked through it until he saw a gravestone reading:

RYAN ALAN GAUTIER

FEB 29 1984

OCT 21 1999

Simon popped up from behind the stone and laughed, "Read the date below, Ryan! It's the day you'll take the grave!"

Ryan turned and ran back to the house. When he saw Marie, she told him, "You have a phone call."

He took the cordless phone and said, "Hello."

"Ryan! I have terrible news!"

"Brett?"

"Yes! It was my mother! Simon electrocuted her!"

"Where are you now?"

"I'm at my cousin Marvin's house."

"Well, I'll probably come see y'all tomorrow."

"That'll be okay."

It was around midnight when Ryan got a call from Kate.

"Hello."

"Is this Ryan?"

"Kate?"

"Yeah."

"How are you?"

"I'm doing good. I just called to see what you were up to."

"I'm not up to much. What about you?"

"I'm reading a horror short-story by Edgar Allan Poe."

"Which one?"

"'Hop-Frog.'"

"That's the one about the midget's revenge."

"That's it."

"I read that one a long time ago."

Kate got a beep. She told Ryan to hold on.

"Hello."

"Hello, Kate," Simon told her from the other line.

"Who's calling?"

"First, you tell me what you're doing and you'll find out."

"I'm reading."

"Reading what?"

"Edgar Allan Poe's 'Hop Frog.'"

"Do you like frogs, Kate?"

"No!"

"Then you oughta love Goliath frogs!"

A humungous, slimy frog squeezed itself through the phone and into Kate's ear. She dropped her cell phone and screamed loudly as a plague of Goliath frogs dropped from the ceiling. She looked to see Simon laughing from the ledge of her window. Shortly, she was soaked in amphibian slime. She ran to the bathroom and took a shower.

"Kate?"

Her mom walked into her room to check on her and saw that she wasn't in there. When she saw Ryan in the high-school courtyard the next morning, Kate told him, "I saw Simon last night!"

"Were you dreaming?"

"No! I was wide awake! He put all these humongous frogs in my room!"

"Are you serious?" Brett asked.

"I'm cemetery-dead serious, Brett!"

"Did one of y'all mention a goblin by the name of Simon?" an unfamiliar voice asked from behind them.

They turned to see a girl having long, red, curly hair and wearing a light-blue sweater and blue jeans.

"Yeah," Kate replied. "And your name is?"

"Wendy Wellborn. I just moved here from Nashville."

"How nice to have you here!" Brett told her.

"Who are you?" she asked him.

"I'm Brett Maker."

"Has Simon been terrorizing your dreams, too?"

"Actually, he attacked me in reality last night."

"I was five when I saw him in my dreams," Wendy told him.

"I was five when he started terrorizing my dreams, too," Ryan told her. "But I overcame him."

"I first encountered him in October 1989," Wendy said.

"I first encountered him in July of that year," Ryan told her.

"What's your name?"

"I'm Ryan Gautier. I just moved here from Duckford, Mississippi."

Then Marvin approached the circle and recognized Wendy as the new face.

"Who are you?" he asked her.

"I'm Wendy, the new girl."

When the bell rang, she told him, "It was nice meeting you-"

"Marvin Maker."

"See ya around, Marvin."

Ryan and Brett went to Ms. Gilberts's class and listened to her talk of the test. She passed it out and told everyone, "Good luck."

Brett was doing very well on the test because he studied for it after all. Suddenly, his paper caught on fire along with his hand. He screamed and caused Ms. Gilberts to stare. He tried to point behind her because Simon was standing on top of the whiteboard, having a yardstick with a very sharp end. When she looked behind herself, she got both of her eyeballs plucked from their sockets. Blood gushed terribly as he stabbed her jaw. All the students ran from the classroom.

"STOP!" Mr. Root yelled in front of them.

After that, Brett recognized Simon standing on his right shoulder.

"Mr. Root!" he yelled as he pointed to him.

He looked to see Simon holding the yardstick aiming at his face. Mr. Root was scared shitless as Simon raised the yardstick up and jammed it into his jaw. He fell into the floor and bled. After that, Simon stabbed his heart numerous times. When the students noticed that their assistant principal was dead, they screamed bloody murder and fled the math hall. The principal Mr. Billy Jo Thomas dismissed everyone to go home for the day and suspended all classes for one week.

Ryan and Brett walked home together. Irving and his football friends were behind them.

"Hey! Look!" Irving shouted. "The gaywot's got a new boyfriend!"

Brett shot up his middle finger and continued walking. What Irving and his friends didn't know was Simon was behind them, holding the blade of an electric saw. He tossed it like a Frisbee at the back of Irving's legs and chopped them off. He fell to the ground and crawled, leaving tracks of blood. Ryan and Brett turned to see Simon standing behind the other boys.

"Now, everyone look how HE walks!" Simon laughed.

Irving's friends were terrified of the evil fiend and ran, leaving him behind. One trucker didn't see him while driving his eighteen-wheeler and accidentally ran over him. Brett stood and began to develop tears from his eyes as he saw his worst enemy die in horrible pain. He didn't want to bother the trucker who got out of his truck and bawled about the accident that he had. Therefore, he and Ryan ran home together.

Ryan began telling Brett about Kate's birthday party and thought about Marvin and the new girl Wendy.

"Is Marvin dating anyone?" he asked Brett.

"He broke up with his girlfriend Lisa this summer. They'd been dating for two years."

"I can talk to Wendy for him."

"Great! He needs a girlfriend. Anyway, what time's Kate's party?"

"Eight."

"Fun."

"Yeah. And her mom won't allow alcohol or drugs."

"I don't smoke at all. I drink every once in a while. But not that much."

Marie came out of the house and said, "Y'all won't believe what I just heard on the radio!"

"What?" Ryan asked.

"There was a seventeen-year-old boy who was ran over and killed by an eighteen-wheeler. When the truck driver saw what he did, he flipped and shot himself! It happened just now!"

"We just saw that boy get killed!" Brett told her.

"But we didn't see the trucker kill himself," Ryan said.

"It's very sad," Brett thought.

"You must be Brett Maker," Marie told him.

"I am."

"Well, Mr. Gautier's at the base right now. He usually gets home late."

"Where all have y'all lived?"

"We're originally from Mississippi. But we've lived in California and Virginia as my husband's been in the military."

Ryan called Kate about Marie cooking dinner. When she arrived, Jean-Claude was home from the naval base.

"Who's the special, young lady?" he asked Ryan.

"Katherine Elizabeth McHenry," she answered. "People call me Kate."

"Hi, Kate. I'm Ryan's dad."

They ate fried chicken and mashed potatoes with brown gravy.

The next night was Kate's "Sweet Sixteen" birthday party. She fixed the backroom up with a puppet of the Cryptkeeper from Tales from the Crypt. She also used a figurine of Freddy Krueger and a figurine of Jason Voorhees. Brett walked Wendy to Marvin and introduced them to each other.

"Hi, Wendy."

"Hi, Marvin."

"Would you care to dance?"

"I'd love to."

Elton John's "Your Song" was playing by the deejay. Marvin and Wendy asked each other questions as they slow-danced together. After a while, Marvin led Wendy out to his car and gave her an ice-cold beer. What the kids didn't know was several neighbors filed complaints on them for causing disturbances in the neighborhood. Craig drove up and caught Marvin and Wendy drinking.

"Excuse me, Marvin," he told him, driving up.

"What's up, Craig?" he asked him.

"May I see your ID?"

Marvin pulled his Tennessee driver's license out for Craig to see. Craig saw that his date of birth was March 21, 1982, and said, "You're still under twenty-one, I see."

Wendy looked to Craig and confessed, "I'm seventeen as well, Craig. I'm sorry."

"Botha y'all step outta the car now!"

When Craig pulled the driver's seat down, a glassed bottle of beer flew up and shattered on his forehead. Nine others flew up and shattered on his forehead as well. He screamed as the blood ran down his face. Simon stood there and laughed at his pain. Craig looked at the goblin and was literally frightened to death. Marvin and Wendy felt that they had to tell everyone the tragic news. He ran to the deejay's booth and asked him to stop the music.

"Everyone, y'all! Craig's dead!" Marvin announced.

"Simon's killed him!" Wendy added.

Everyone except Ryan, Kate, and Brett were laughing until they saw a log roll from the fireplace and set most of the downstairs area on fire. Kate watched Simon standing on the chandelier.

"Please, stop!" she begged, having tears from her blue eyes.

Then Simon broke the chandelier, causing it to fall onto several of her longtime friends. They fell to the floor and died as they were electrocuted. The other guests were running for their lives. A fire engine zoomed to the scene.

On Monday morning, a local reporter talked of the bizarre and mysterious events that occurred in Raven's Stone that weekend. She mentioned that Mr. Root and a quarter of the students at Raven's Stone High weren't around anymore. Later that afternoon, Marvin took Wendy and showed her his poolroom.

He remembered that he had to get another poolstick.

"I'll be right back," he told her.

"Okay."

He discovered that it was very slippery around where he hung his poolsticks. He slipped backward and fell outside his glassed window, shattering it and cutting his back. He landed into a silver vat of quicksand that Simon had put out there for him. Wendy became discouraged several minutes later. She walked downstairs and asked Dorothy Maker, Marvin's mom, "Mrs. Maker, have you seen Marvin?"

"I thought y'all were together in the poolroom," Dorothy said.

"We were. But then he went to his room for something and never came back."

"That's weird."

Wendy walked home after that.

Ryan heard his phone ring and answered it by saying, "Hello."

"Ryan?"

"Brett?"

"Ryan! Marvin's missing!"

"What the hell?"

"He just walked into his room and disappeared!"

"That's crazy!"

"You're telling me."

All that evening, Kate was sad for Marvin. It was around eleven when she got into the shower and shampooed her hair. When she finished showering, she got out and wrapped a camouflage towel around herself and looked into the bathroom. That was when she saw Simon behind her.

"I hope you and Ryan have a long wedding-shower," he told her. "Because it sure as hell is gonna be a short honeymoon."

She was so frightened when she saw that he had a silver pail of boiling lava. She dodged when he tried to throw it on her. The towel fell off of her as she ran outside the front door.

She ran to Ryan's house. He and Brett were looking outside the window as she was coming up to the porch. He swung the door opened and said, "Kate! My mom's gonna have a heart attack!"

"What the hell happened to you, Katherine Elizabeth McHenry?" Brett asked.

"What the hell does it look like, Brett Aaron Maker? Some psychotic goblin just tried to kill me in the shower!"

Ryan ran to get a blue robe for her. He tossed it to her. She fastened it as she heard Marie coming into the room.

"Ryan Alan Gautier! What the hell's going on?"

"Mom, it's not what you think! I promise!"

Then they heard a knock on the door. Ryan answered and saw a Raven's Stone officer standing there. He was an Asian foreigner.

"You!" he snapped, pointing his finger at Kate.

"Me?" Kate guessed.

"You! Come here!"

Kate walked to him and listened him say, "Thirty-seven degrees far too cold for streaking. I let it slide this time only. Next time, you busted. Understand? Or I speak Vietnamese and don't notice me self?"

"Yes, sir," she replied.

The officer left and drove away.

"I'm sorry, Kate," Brett told her. "I couldn't arrest you for streaking. I'd probably stick my head out the window and how like a coyote."

"Very funny!" she snarled.

After that, Brett's cell phone rang. He took it from his coat and couldn't believe that it was Marvin calling. He reluctantly answered it by saying, "Hello."

"Brett?"

"Marvin, where the hell have you been?"

"I fell in a vat of quicksand and escaped. It took me an hour to do it."

"No way in hell!"

"I did. And I'm not in hell. Thank God! You need to call Wendy and tell her."

"I don't think she'll understand."

"I guess you're right."

"I'm so glad you're alright, Marvin."

"So am I."

"Thanks for calling."

"You're welcomed."

After the cousins hung up, Marvin looked to see Simon.

"You won't be okay for long!"

"Holy shit!"

Simon violently forced a torch into his face and set him on fire. Brett and Wendy found Marvin's horribly burned body just an hour later. Brett barfed like a cocker spaniel. Wendy wept bitterly.

"Hello, kids," Simon said from behind them.

They quickly turned around as Wendy told him, "You're going down, Simon!"

"You better think twice about that, Wendy," Simon told her.

He snapped his fingers and summoned a pushing lawnmower that zoomed out of Marvin's closet. It chased Brett outside a two-story window. He broke his right arm and screamed in grave pain. The lawnmower zoomed over him, slicing open many of his veins. He bled heavily.

"BRETT!" Wendy screamed in horror.

She ran for her life and saw Kate sitting with Ryan on his front porch. She could see that Wendy was upset and asked, "What's wrong?"

"The Maker boys are dead!"

"What the hell?" Ryan wondered.

"Simon did it!"

Jean-Claude drove up and saw what was going on.

"What the hell's going on?"

"Our friends were killed, Dad," Ryan answered.

"Killed?"

"They were murdered by some evil goblin. And no. I'm not insane."

"What goblin?"

"Simon," Wendy answered.

"Simon's dead," Jean-Claude snapped.

"Not anymore," Simon said, popping up from the porch's floor.

Kate turned to see him and smiled flawlessly.

"Kate?" Wendy wondered.

"No, Simon," Ryan told him.

"You're no longer a threat to me, either. I believe in Jesus. I believe in Santa Claus. I believe in the Easter Bunny. I even believe in the Tooth Fairy. But you're just fake. You're not even real."

He tossed a bottle of kerosene onto Simon and struck a red cigarette-lighter on Simon's face, setting him on fire. Simon screamed bloody murder and stomped like Rumpelstiltskin in the end of the ancient fairytale and vanished.

Ryan, Kate, and Wendy embraced each other in grief over their lost friends. Through their last years of school, their friends came and went. Many survivors of the terrible bloodbath were haunted by the memory of Simon in their nightmares and were committed to the psychiatric clinic at Nashville State Hospital.

EERIE OCTOBER

Only the dead have seen the end of the war.
Plato

Tim and Zach decided to stay at their dorms and study for their midterms on the night of Friday, October 8, 2004. To avoid all distractions, Zach turned everything off-including his cell phone. At around eleven-thirty, he heard his phone ring. He reluctantly answered it by saying, "Hello."

"Zach?" a female voice whispered from the other line.

"Veronica? I was thinking you were asleep! For Christ sake, it's almost midnight!"

"I was wondering if you would like to meet me at the cemetery at midnight."

"The cemetery?"

"Yeah. Gibson Valley City Cemetery."

"You sure about that?"

"I'm positive."

"Okay," he sighed.

"I'll see you there at twelve o'clock sharp. Don't keep me waiting. Or you'll be sorry."

"Yes, ma'am."

After he hung up, Zach picked up The Complete Tales and Poems of Edgar Allan Poe, the book that he borrowed from the college library, and turned in it to read "The Cask of Amontillado." After reading Poe's premature-burial tale for around twenty minutes, he put the book down and left the dorm.

He went out and jogged through the small-town silence of Gibson Valley. When he got to the cemetery, he saw Veronica nowhere.

"I'm over here, Zach!" a female voice called for him inside the cemetery.

He ran through the gate and saw that the young woman, who was standing in front of a grave, looked exactly like Veronica from where he was standing. When he got close enough, he saw that she wasn't Veronica. After she vanished, he slipped and found himself in a pit with a skeleton. As he climbed out of the pit, he saw two shadows walking toward him and thought, "Dammit!"

"Zach?" his black friend Malachi wondered.

"That's me."

"Who the hell you think you are? Ed Gein?" Zeke, Malachi's twin brother, asked.

"Ed Gein was one sick bastard!" Zach declared.

"So are you! If you cummin to the cemetery after midnight and diggin' up somebody's grave! Ain't you got respect for the dead?"

"I gotta call somebody bout this!" Malachi laughed. "We gonna have so much fun, laughin' bout this at school Monday!"

When Malachi pressed a digit on his cell phone, he heard a gun cock at the side of his head. He and Zeke looked to see a Union troop frowning at them as he was aiming a rifle at them.

"What the hell?" Zeke wondered.

"What the hell what?" Zach asked.

The Union troop had came and went before he could even blink his eyes.

"We just saw a damn ghost!" Malachi said. "We shoulda gotta pitcha that!"

Then all boys began hearing rifles shooting from behind them. They looked to see Union troops firing from the gravestones in the back of the cemetery. They jumped to the ground to dodge the bullets. After the gunshots, they heard sirens.

"Is that the cops or an ambulance?" Zeke wondered.

"Who knows?" Zach thought.

They heard people walk into the cemetery and trot toward them.

"What the hell y'all kids doing?" Officer Mike Jeffcoat snapped. He flashed his flashlight on them.

"It's a long story, sir," Zach answered, trying his best to explain.

"Don't give me that bullshit! Just tell me what the hell happened!"

"I came here to meet several friends of mine, Mr. Jeffcoat. And I just, outta the blue, landed in a grave! Apparently, there's been a grave robbery in town."

"What the hell y'all kids playing in the cemetery after midnight for?" Jeffcoat asked.

Zach shrugged his shoulders and came up with an excuse that was probably ancient before Egypt was discovered: "I don't know."

Then they heard the cry of an infant child as they saw pink orbs rise near the graves and a younger woman singing, "Hush, little baby. Don't say a word."

Jeffcoat flashed his light on the bench onto the corner at the other end of the cemetery. He and the two other officers walked toward her.

"Ma'am, you're gonna have to take that baby and go somewhere else," Jeffcoat told her.

She only ignored him and continued humming. When they got close enough, she and the baby vanished. They saw two black ravens sipping blood from the stone bench where she was sitting. Jeffcoat looked to the boys and said, "Y'all boys. I don't care where y'all go when y'all leave here. But I want y'all to go now. And I don't wanna see any of y'all back here unless y'all come to us for permission. Am I clear?"

"Yes, sir!"

When they got back to the college, they saw Craig, the head resident, smoking a cigarette on the porch of James Hall.

"What the hell's wrong with y'all?" he asked them.

"We just went to hell and came back!" Malachi answered as he was out of breath.

"Y'all look like y'all seen a ghost."

"Not just one!" Zach told him.

"I'll believe that bullshit when I see it!"

"Suit yourself," Zeke told him.

"I will."

Then a large, silver cannon rolled on wheels around the curves and fired cannons. The four guys ran inside the hall and got into their dorms. Zach locked his door and couldn't sleep until four o'clock in the morning.

Hours later, he woke up by a loud knock on his door.

"Who's there?" he moaned.

"It's Tim!"

"I'll be right there!"

He walked to the door and slowly answered it.

"Hell, Zach! It's after twelve. Where the hell you been all day?"

"I've been asleep. I couldn't get any last night."

"Why the hell not?"

"Can you say cemetery?"

"Zach, you had to have been dreaming. I didn't hear you even leave your dorm last night."

"I was very quiet about it."

"Whatever you say."

"That is whatever I say."

"I won't argue."

"Good."

"Let's go get some lunch at Taco Bell," Tim insisted.

"I'd love an ice-cold Mountain Dew and steak chalupa."

"Then let's go."

When they walked outside, it was peaceful around James Hall. There weren't many people around. Zach got into Tim's car. When Tim put the car in gear, the boys began to see the cannon roll around the corner of James Hall.

"Holy shit!" Zach shrieked.

Tim sped up. When he recognized the cannon firing a cannon toward his car, he and Zach jumped out of the car. He was unspeakably furious to see that his car was in critical condition. Then the cannon rolled into the street and fired at vehicles and pedestrians that were passing by. Some were struck by the cannonballs; left severely wounded or even dead. Tim and Zach completely lost their appetites.

It was that evening when Zach got a call from Tim.

"What's going on, Zach?"

"Not much, Tim."

"We're wanting to take Mindy out for her birthday tonight at the Olive Garden. She wants you to come with us. It's gonna be me, her, and her friends from the dance team."

"I'd love to! I gotta tell Veronica. She'll probably wanna go, too."

"We're gonna be there at seven."

"It's five now."

"That means we have two hours."

"I'm gonna call her. Just as soon as I get off the phone with you."

"I'll see y'all then."

"You bet."

Two hours later, they were at Olive Garden for Tim's girlfriend Mindy's birthday. They munched on breadsticks with marinara sauce as Zach told them, "Y'all will not believe what happened to me last night round eleven-thirty."

"What?" Mindy asked anxiously.

"You know about Gibson Valley City Cemetery, right?"

"Yeah. Is it really haunted?"

"I'm glad you asked," Zach told her. "Because I got a prank pulled on me by a ghost there last night. I ended up falling in a grave. Then Malachi and Zeke, you know, the McClendon twins."

"Yeah," Mindy nodded.

"They showed up. And I thought they were the damn cops. Scared the hell outta me! Malachi started laughing and got his cell phone out, wanting to brag to someone about it. That was when he and Zeke said a ghost threatened them with a gun."

"We so gotta see that!" Veronica thought.

"Veronica! No!" Zach told her.

"Zach! Yes!"

"Let's go after dinner," Mindy insisted.

Zach and Tim rolled their eyes.

An hour later, the teens were walking in the cemetery.

"Show us where you fell in that grave!" Mindy told him.

"Follow me if you wanna know," Zach told her.

She and the other girls followed her. When they got there, they saw that the grave was reburied.

"I think you're lying!" Veronica snapped in disappointment.

"I swear!"

Then Veronica heard a gun cock at the side of her head. She quickly turned to see a Union troop standing there, frowning at her as he was aiming a rifle at her face. She was frightened to tears as she jumped back. After he vanished, the cannon rolled up the hill. There was a Union troop riding it as he shouted to them by their names and shouted to them, "Never return!"

THE HOUSE OF GOMORRAH FALLS

1: DAVID CLARK'S MOVE

David sat at the phone in his bedroom where he was living at his parents' home in Duckford, Mississippi. He was talking with his longtime friend Leah.

"You know, Leah, I don't know if you remember me telling you I'm a philosophy fan."

"Yeah."

"Well, this philosopher once said that everyone becomes a poet at the touch of love."

"Nietzsche?"

"Actually, it was Plato. And I was inspired to write a poem about my and your dance at Sadie Hawkins 2004. Let me read it to you."

"Okay."

He read it to her. When he was finished, she said, "That was absolutely beautiful."

"It was entitled 'The Touch of a Friend's Love.'"

"I like it. I bet you're gonna have money coming outta your ears after that poem's published."

79

"That'd be great. But I don't count my chickens before they hatch."

"That's good. Are you saved, David?"

"Yes."

"You've made Jesus your personal Savior?"

"I did when I was thirteen in late 2000. What about you?"

"I accepted the Lord when I was very young, too. I was listening to Ray Boltz sing a song called 'Thank You.'"

"I've heard some of his music."

"He's really good."

Suddenly, he changed the subject by asking, "Do you plan to go to college anywhere?"

"I'm actually going to Yankee Land for college."

"Let me guess; you're going to Harvard to become a lawyer."

"Not even close."

"Okay," she laughed.

"It's White Mountain Community College in Gomorrah Falls, New Hampshire. I've planned to become an English teacher."

"Did I tell you what I plan to become?"

"No. What?"

"I'm planning to major in business."

"Good luck."

"You, too, David. Let's keep in touch."

"Okay. Bye."

"Bye, David. Take care."

The summer break was ended for David in late August. He and his parents Darrel and Sheila Clark were loading a silver car as Rod Stewart's "Forever Young," the class song, played on the radio. Then he shook his dad's hand and kissed his mom goodbye. He spent the night in Pigeon Forge, Tennessee; Baltimore, and Boston. Finally, he made it to Gomorrah Falls, New Hampshire. When he got out of his car, he saw a blond, curly-haired, young man standing there.

"You're a long way from home," he said.

"I guess you could say that. I'm David. Just like the Hebrew boy who slew the Philistine giant Goliath."

"I'm Michael McNairy. My first name's mentioned in Revelation. Michael's the archangel who'll chain Satan to the giant stone in a bottomless pit for a thousand years. So, how did you hear of this place?"

"I read about it in something and enrolled over the Internet. I know I read a lot."

"What do you read?"

"Mainly fiction. I'm a real reader of Edgar Allan Poe."

"Poe was brilliant."

"Many writers became followers of Poe. Know who HP Lovecraft was?"

"Yeah. Stephen King imitated Lovecraft in his story 'Jerusalem's Lot' in his collection Night Shift."

"I actually read a story in that book one time. It wasn't that one though. And I have read several of Lovecraft's works. He wrote in a very similar tone to Poe's."

"I have The Best of HP Lovecraft: Black Seas of Infinity if you'd like to borrow it sometime."

"Sure," Michael said as a young lady, having long, brown, curly hair, walked up beside him.

"Sarah, this is David."

"Hey, Sarah."

"I bet you're from Tulsa," she said.

"Oklahoma?"

"Yeah."

"No, but you mighta seen me out there dropping off a loada Salsa."

Sarah burst into laughter and asked, "What song was that?"

"'Where I Come From' by Alan Jackson."

"I see you're a music buff."

"Some people have thought that of me."

"You need to meet my best friend," she said.

"What's she like?" David asked.

"First of all, her name's Naomi Longfellow. She's a blue-eyed redhead. And she's very nice. You'd like her. She really loves Southern movies."

"I gotta meet this girl!"

"I'll talk to her for you."

"Thank you very much."

"Can you say it like Elvis?" she asked.

David did his best impersonation of the King. Sarah laughed and said, "Naomi loves Elvis! You should see her room!"

"Well, take me to meet her!" David said anxiously.

"She's at work right now," Sarah answered.

"Where?"

"She's a waitress at Buffalo Wild Wings," Michael answered.

"I bet she doesn't get off till late," David thought.

"She usually doesn't," Sarah said.

"Well, I'm gonna go unload my car and go find my dorm, y'all."

Michael and Sarah giggled. Then Michael asked, "What's your name?"

"Clark."

"Guess what! You're rooming with me, this black boy Josh, and Cain, whose family came over here from Cambodia."

"Cambodia in Southeast Asia?"

"Yeah. And he plans to get a Doctor of Medicine title."

"He must be smart."

"He is that. He's awesome at math."

"Oh, I was miserable at algebra and geometry."

"You're not alone."

"Thanks for the reassurance."

As the two walked into the living area of the dormitory, Michael announced, "Boys, this is the Southern exchange student David Clark!"

David just grinned as Sarah and the two boys laughed. When they were quiet, he said, "Hey, y'all."

"What's up?" Josh asked.

"For me, I just got into my dorm. I'm seeing new people in a new place. This is practically a new world because I'm not from the North."

"I can tell you about being in a strange country," Cain said.

"Michael told me you came over here from Cambodia."

"I came over here from there with my parents and two older brothers in July 1992. I was only five and couldn't speak English at all."

"You know, I read about Cambodia under Pol Pot and the Khmer Rouge. He was a terrible man."

"He was," Cain agreed. "And I'll be honest; I don't like being named for a murderer."

"Are you a Christian?" David asked.

"I am."

"I know that Buddhism is a major religion in Cambodia."

"It is."

Then Sarah announced, "I'm going to my dorm, you guys."

"Goodnight," the boys told her.

She kissed Michael's lips on her way out the door and whispered, "Goodnight, honey."

"I love you," he whispered.

2: DAVID AND NAOMI MEET

It was the morning of Tuesday, September 5, 2006, when David woke up and overlooked his schedule. He had Mr. James McLemore for world history at eight. He had Mr. John Winchell for English at ten. He had Mrs. Veronica Moat for a math class at one. Lastly, he had Mrs. Deborah Hayes for a science class at three. He looked at his clock and saw that it was seven-twenty. He went and got ready for the day.

He was sitting in his first-hour class when he watched a redhead walk in with Sarah. Heaven knew what all she was talking about. Her long, red hair was down. She was wearing a pair of glasses. Her black shirt was of the Beatles. She was wearing a pair of blue-jean shorts along with a pair of leather sandals. She and Sarah approached him.

"David," Sarah said. "This is Naomi Longfellow."

"Hi, David," Naomi said as she sat in the seat behind him.

"Hi, Naomi. Great shirt."

"Thanks! The Beatles rock!"

"Sarah said you love Elvis."

"I do. My mom told me of how she remembers that she was eighteen on the day that he died. And she was so upset!"

"There were a lotta people upset when he died. And I'm sure a lotta teen girls were upset, too."

"I couldn't doubt it."

Then Mr. McLemore walked into the classroom.

"We'll talk more later," David whispered.

"Okay."

After Mr. McLemore dismissed the class at nine-thirty, David and Naomi walked into the hall together.

"Believe it or not, I'm from Elvis's home state."

"You're from Tennessee?"

"Mississippi. That was where he was born on January 8, 1935."

"Wait! I knew that!"

"Naomi, what's your middle name?"

"Ann."

"Naomi Ann. That is so pretty."

"Thank you."

"You're very welcomed. Have you read Ruth in the Bible?"

"Yeah. That's who my mom named me for. Because her name is Barbara Ruth."

"Naomi was Ruth's mother-in-law."

"Yes, she was. Now, what about you? What's your middle name?"

"Isaac. David Isaac Clark."

"Isaac was offered as a sacrifice to God by his father Abraham but was spared at the last moment."

"You know, I couldn't believe the name of this name of this town."

"I know. Out-of-towners ask us questions like if we're all bad people like murderers, rapists, pedophiles, dope fiends."

"What do you tell them?"

"I say that not everyone of Gomorrah Falls is like that."

"Of course not. There were probably good people of Sodom and Gomorrah, too. Not just Lot and his family."

"I guess you're right."

"Well, I know a lotta good people suffered Katrina in New Orleans."

"Were you a Katrina victim?"

"My parents and I evacuated to Tennessee."

"I'm sorry to hear that."

"The Lord blessed us. We came home from my sister's house and found ours back in one piece."

"That is a blessing."

Then David changed the subject by asking, "Don't you work at Buffalo Wild Wings?"

"Yes," she replied, nodding.

"What time do you go in for work?"

"One. And I gotta get to class. Here's my number. Gimme your hand."

She took a blue pen and wrote the ten digits on the back of his hand.

"You better call me," she said.

"I will. Does this mean yes?"

"What?"

"You will go out with me?"

"I will."

David couldn't believe what he was hearing. Naomi was smiling as she was looking into his hazel eyes. She embraced his neck and hugged him. People were watching as they walked by.

"I gotta go to class now!" they said to each other and ran.

"I think Naomi's in love," Sarah told Michael.

"I'd be happy for her. I'm not getting my hopes up. They just met."

"He won't propose anytime soon. That is, of course, if he has sense."

It was that evening when David sat in his room, reading "At the Mountains of Madness" by HP Lovecraft. He suddenly thought, "I need to call Naomi."

He dialed her cell-phone number and heard her answer the second ring.

"Hello."

"Naomi?"

"Is this David?"

"Yes, it is."

"Hey, boy! Called me at the right time. I'm on my break now."

"Well, you said I'd better call you."

"That's right. What are you doing tonight?"

"Me? I'm probably not doing anything."

"I have an idea where we can go."

"Where?"

"It's a vacant house down the road from the college. Vacant for years. The widow was very old when she was found dead in it. She was survived by her two sons who've been wanting to rent the house out to anyone. The reason that they can't is the terrifying legend surrounding the place."

"How's it go?"

"The old woman had a pet Siberian husky that killed the varmints that came in the yard. Over the years since she died, people have snuck on the property and witnessed terrible demons that looked to be possums, raccoons, squirrels with horns, wings, and speared tails along with rows of teeth like sharks."

"Scary place."

"You up for it?"

"Sure."

"Great. Now, I gotta get back to work. See you around nine-thirty."

"Bye."

"Bye, David."

3: AHAB

Several hours later, David heard a knock on his door.

"Who's there?"

"It's Naomi."

"Come in."

She opened the door and walked in.

"Hey, girl!"

"Hey!"

She heard Ronny Milsap singing "Smoky Mountain Rain" on the radio.

"So, David," she said.

"Yes."

"Tell me about the South."

"Well, it's different down there. I mean, we don't marry our cousins at sixteen and raise twelve kids on a goat farm. I don't know anyone who's dated their our own relatives. It's a myth."

"I'd hope so."

"I haven't heard people say y'all up here at all."

"So it is different up here after all."

"That's true."

"Well, are you ready to go?"

"Sure," he sighed.

David walked with Naomi to her red Mustang. When he sat in the front, he heard Confederate Railroad's "Elvis and Andy" on her stereo.

"You know of Confederate Railroad?" he asked.

"Yes! They were great!"

"I've heard this song many times and I love it!"

"I think it's my theme song. I bet if I went to Mississippi, you all would think I was a Southern belle."

"It's y'all."

"Oh, yeah."

She suddenly turned to the right and drove down Amos Mott Road until she was in front of a house that had NO TRESPASSING posted in front of it. She put the car in park and said, "Let's go."

They got out of the car and walked into the backyard until they saw a skinless rodent say, "His name is Ahab. And he loves to feed on the blood of humans."

"Holy shit!" David shrieked as he and Naomi jumped back.

"Leave while you still can," the rodent warned.

The two began to feel a cold breeze pick up from the backyard.

"This is too weird," Naomi thought as she became uncomfortable.

"I was thinking the same thing," David thought.

"Well, let's go!"

They got into the car. Naomi sped away back to the college. After they told each other goodnight, David ran back to his dorm and saw the boys gathered in the living area, watching television.

"What's happening, man?" Josh asked.

"Y'all won't believe this!" he announced.

"Did you and Naomi have sex?" Michael asked.

"Hell no!"

"What happened?" Cain asked anxiously.

"We went to this place on Amos Mott Road. That place is beyond evil!"

"That place has been rumored to be demonic," Michael said. " And Sam Mott, who lives around there and owns that property, will call the law on you if he catches you trespassing on it. His grandparents lived in that house until they died years ago."

"So, the old widow was his grandma?" David guessed.

"Martha Mott was his grandmother. That's correct."

"Naomi told me about her living there with her pet Siberian husky that killed the varmints in the yard. Then they found her dead inside that house. Now, they can't rent it out to anyone because of those rumors of the place being demonic."

"I think they're full of shit," Josh thought.

After that, he got up and walked out to the porch of Cartland Hall. He lit a cigar and puffed until he saw Ahab, a grotesque demon in form of a possum having red fur and wings, golden horns, rows of teeth like a shark, and a long speared tail, fly up and snarl, "Who's full of shit now, bitch?"

He was absolutely spooked out. He knew that he smoked only several cigars a day. He didn't drink that much. He never took drugs illegally. All his life, he believed that there was one Ghost. Josh believed in Him as the Holy Ghost.

Ahab was growling at him like a vicious Rottweiler guarding a junkyard as he could read Josh's mind. He was reading the Rev. Perry McElven's sermon one Sunday morning. He told Ahab, "You're no threat to me, demon! Because I've been covered by the precious blood of the Lamb!"

Ahab hissed like a vicious snake and attacked Josh before he was able to get away. He scratched his face, leaving deep scars as well as he bit his neck. Then he flew away before anyone could see him. The residents of Cartland Hall ran out there to see that Josh had died a brutal and gruesome death. After being pronounced Dead at the Scene, the paramedics hauled his bloody corpse away. The tragic news got around campus quickly the next morning, shocking everyone. Sarah, Naomi, and other girls were in tears.

Rev. McElven officiated the funeral at Cross of Calvary Holiness Church. While Josh's cousin Milton sang Master P's "I Miss My Homie," everyone began weeping. David was sitting with Naomi, Sarah, Cain, and Michael on one of the pews on the back. They were several of the only white people inside the church. David wasn't a racist at all. But he felt uncomfortable when he'd go somewhere and be the only white person there even though he knew not all blacks were bad; not all whites were good. When he got in the car with Naomi after leaving the burial service at the graveyard, he told her, "I wish I woulda got to know him better."

"He was a good guy. I'm really gonna miss him."

"I wonder who the murderer coulda been."

"God knows. And they're gonna have to answer to Him for it. I know that much."

"That's right."

Then she changed the subject by saying, "David, I know you haven't met my family yet."

"No."

"Well, how about tonight?"

"Tonight?"

"Tonight at Kobayashi's."

"Where's that?"

"You can ride with me. It's a sushi bar and Chinese restaurant. The workers are Chinese, Japanese, Korean, and Vietnamese."

"They must know what it was like for the people building the Tower of the Babel. I know they're all Asians. But they speak different languages."

"They can speak English."

"Can you understand them talk?"

"Somewhat?"

Suddenly, they were on campus.

"I'll see you tonight," she told him.

It was around seven when David and Naomi arrived at Kobayashi's and walked inside the restaurant.

"Is it just you two?" the small, Asian lady, who was standing by the counter, asked.

"We're meeting some people here," Naomi told her, smiling.

"Okay," the lady told her, smiling. "Enjoy."

They noticed the table where her parents Tim and Ruth and her younger brother Matt were sitting.

"Hey, y'all," David told them.

"Y'all?" Ruth guessed.

"David's from Mississippi, Mom," Naomi explained.

"I am," he admitted. "And that's only a myth."

"What?" Tim wondered.

"I never knew anyone who dated their cousin or married them at sixteen and raised twelve kids on a goat farm."

Tim chuckled and said, "I understand. I've read works from several Southern authors: William Faulkner, John Grisham, Tennessee Williams, Eudora Welty, Truman Capote."

"I like to read."

"So do I."

After that, they went to fill their plates.

David learned what Tim and Ruth did for a living. He was an attorney and a fan of John Grisham's books. He had a shelf full of Grisham's books above his computer at their two-story house. Ruth taught English at Gomorrah Falls High. She was a fan of Stephen King. She'd been collecting his books since his novel Carrie was published in 1974. David found Naomi's parents interesting. Her brother Matt was of the baseball team at Gomorrah Falls High and in his sophomore year. He was a fan of the Boston Red Sox and planning to attend Harvard and become a Doctor of Medicine.

After dinner, Naomi asked David, "What did you think of my family?"

"They're very nice. Y'all have been very nice to me up here."

"Not what you expected?"

"Not everything I expected."

Then he moved her long, red hair back and kissed her lips.

"I love you," he whispered.

"I love you."

They went to their rooms inside their dorms. Both turned their radios and heard "Summer Nights" from the movie Grease. Suddenly, David noticed that Michael was nowhere in sight. Naomi noticed that Sarah was nowhere in their dorm as well.

Michael and Sarah tiptoed into the lawn of the vacant house as they both looked at their watches and saw that it was almost nine. It was very dark around there. Before they could blink, dark-red orbs began floating in the air. There were suddenly more than they could count. A powerfully cold wind began to blow on the lawn as well as the orbs struck their faces. They found that the orbs were gaseous. Their faces became burned and scarred. When they opened their eyes, they saw Ahab flying toward them.

"Let's go!" Sarah snapped.

When they got back to the college, they rushed to Michael's dorm.

"Holy shit!" Cain shrieked with his mouth dropped.

"We went!" Sarah said.

"It was hell!" Michael swore.

"What it looks like," David thought.

"That's one place I'll never go back," Sarah said out of breath.

"Did you see Ahab? Y'all?" David asked.

"Who?" Michael asked.

"He's a winged possum with red fur and rows of teeth like a shark," David answered.

"Are you doing LSD, David?" Cain asked.

"We saw him, too!" Michael swore. "And I don't do any of that shit at all!"

"Ahab!" Cain laughed. "That's an Arabic name! You think Osama bin Laden's been to hell, manipulating demons to join al-Qaeda?"

David and Michael looked at him for a moment and thought, "Good one!"

"I'll see you guys later," Sarah sighed, rolling her eyes.

She walked into her dorm. That was when Naomi shrieked, "Sarah! What the hell did you do to yourself?"

"And saw Ahab, the demon possum?"

"Unfortunately."

"He come after you?"

"He did. But he beat me and Michael to the car."

"Praise You, God!" Naomi sighed. "I pray this in the precious name of Your Son Jesus. Amen."

"Can say that again."

"You're starting to sound like you're from Dixie," Sarah said.

"Damn right. When I saw David, I knew it right then and there. If heaven ain't like Dixie, I don't wanna go."

After she said that, Ahab flew through the window, shattering it. The girls both squealed. Then he said, "I'll just take you to the Deeper South. It's more like hell!"

He turned to see what Naomi had on the shelf; a figurine of Jesus. He knocked it off and laughed as it shattered when it hit the floor.

"You son of a bitch!" Naomi screamed.

"I'm nowhere near done," Ahab declared.

He flew into the shelf and knocked Naomi's copy of The Passion of the Christ on DVD off. Then he broke it. She burst into tears.

"You remember the Bible, don't you?" Sarah asked her.

"Yeah."

"Rebuke the enemy and he shall flee."

Ahab became furious and flew into Sarah. He bit her neck, inflicting horrible pain. Then she fell to the floor and bled to death. Ahab burst into laughter like Bela Lugosi would in his role of the demented villain in one of those ancient horror-movies. Then he flew away. Jared, a security guard, ran in along with Joel, another security guard.

"Holy Jesus!" Jared shrieked as he saw Sarah's corpse.

"It wasn't even human!" Naomi swore.

"What?" Joel asked.

"The murderer!"

"Doesn't look like it," Jared thought. "Looks as if it could've been a vampire with those damn marks on her neck."

"Jared, stop playing!" Joel snapped.

"It didn't have to be a vampire or werewolf or any of that other shit," Jared told him.

Then he noticed the shattered window and thought, "Damn! Now, I know that the son of a bitch couldn't have been human!"

"He came through that window!" Naomi swore. "He was a pure evil demon!"

Joel rolled his eyes.

"That's enough! Now, can you describe the murderer?"

"He was a red possum with wings. He broke my Jesus figurine and my DVD of The Passion. He was purely evil!"

"He must be an inhabitant of that place on Amos Mott Road," Jared thought.

"I saw him there. I was with David Clark. He recently moved here from Mississippi."

"And if I'm not mistaking, this is the body of Sarah Elizabeth Steelman," Jared guessed.

"Yes. She was my best friend for years and Michael McNairy's fiancée."

"We'll tell him."

"Let me."

"Okay."

"Thank you."

She walked over to Cartland Hall and knocked on their dorm. Michael answered and saw her there.

"Sarah," she whispered.

"What happened?"

"She's dead."

"No!"

"It was Ahab."

"Thanks, Naomi," he sighed.

He went back into the dorm and said, "You guys."

David and Cain looked to him.

"Ahab's killed Sarah."

"No way!" Cain said in shock.

"I think it's time to put that big dog to sleep for good!" Michael declared.

It was the stroke of midnight when David drove to the vacant house and saw the Rev. McElven standing there.

"I've been expecting you, David."

"Who are you?"

"I'm the Rev. Perry McElven. I'm here on the Lord's work."

"Okay."

He held out a red bag and said, "These are five stones from the shores of Galilee."

"Do I toss them at Ahab's head to kill him?"

"That's correct. Then you'll have another fish to fry: Omar, the violet raccoon-demon."

"I'll be ready."

"I talked to God. And He told me you'll be just fine."

"Thank you."

"You're welcomed."

After that, Rev. McElven wished David the best of luck and left. Then Ahab flew into sight. David threw the first stone and struck his forehead. He screamed in pain. David threw the other four stones and struck the fiend in the same place. Ahab fell to the ground and was nevermore.

4: OMAR'S FIERCE WRATH

It was the morning of Friday, October 13, 2006, when David woke up to Brewer & Shipley singing "One Toke over the Line" on the radio. He saw that it was a quarter after six. Then his cell phone rang. He looked and saw that it was Naomi calling. He answered and said, "Good morning, sweetie."

"Good morning, honey."

"How are you?"

"I'm very well. Would you like to go out for breakfast at Donut Time."

"I love donuts."

"It's all on me."

"You are too sweet. Sugar's got nothing on you."

"I was elected 'Sweetest Female Student' in my sophomore year at Gomorrah Falls High."

"You are the sweetest."

"I know. That's why you love me."

"Damn right."

"Okay. I'll see you at Donut Time."

When he arrived there, he saw Naomi getting out of her car. She smiled and told him, "Hey, boy."

"Hey, sweetie."

They kissed each other's lips. Inside the restaurant, they ordered a box of a dozen fudge-glazed donuts and medium glasses of orange juice. After they both finished, David put two ones on the table for Hannah, their waitress.

"You guys, have a good day," she told them as she watched them walk outside the door.

When they got outside, they ran into one of Naomi's former classmates by the name of Rachel Mott. She was elected "Most Likely to Succeed" and the valedictorian. She was the youngest of Samuel and Oprah Mott's four children.

Naomi was shocked to see her not smiling at all. She looked at David and her and said, "I know what you were up to that night."

"What the hell are you even trying to say, Rachel?"

"Omar's wrath is fierce. Be very afraid."

"Thanks for the warning," Naomi said sarcastically.

Both of them went back on campus and prepared for the day. David saw Michael and Cain in the living area and asked, "Do y'all know a Rachel Mott?"

"Yeah," they replied.

"Naomi and I saw her at the donut place just a while ago. She told us to beware of Omar's fierce wrath."

"Omar?" Cain wondered.

"I'm sure she was full of horseshit like a damn barnhouse," Michael thought.

"Besides, Omar's an Arabic name," David said. "Do y'all think she could be involved with the terrorists?"

"She's an American," Michael said.

"Osama bin Laden's got people from all around the globe," David said. "And I like to compare the American ones to Benedict Arnold."

"You're right, Dave," Cain said.

After he ate lunch, David began to remember something while leaving the cafeteria. He remembered Rev. McElven's warning of Omar weeks earlier.

"Dammit!"

He began to know how all the people felt after they watched God slam the door on the Ark and realize that Noah wasn't insane after all. He ran inside his room and dialed Naomi's phone number. She answered the third ring.

"Hello."

"Naomi! I just remembered!"

"What?"

"Rachel Mott's not insane!"

"What are you saying?"

"Rev. Perry McElven told me of Omar. He's a purple-furred, winged, demonic raccoon!"

"Rev. McElven, the black preacher?"

"That's right!"

"Hey, David, I gotta get ready for work."

"Okay."

"Bye, honey."

"I love you."

They hung up. When he saw Michael and Cain later, David told them, "I understand what Rachel meant about the wrath of Omar."

"What?" Michael asked after he took a sip of beer.

"The old house that's been abandoned for years. He's an inhabitant of the surrounding area of it."

"I'm going to see for myself," Michael said as he took the last sip.

He'd been drinking heavily since Sarah died. David expected him to come back (if he came back alive) with a wild story to tell. He was in the lobby of Cartland Hall when he saw Rachel.

"Michael McNairy!"

"May I help you, Rachel Mott?"

"When you get where you're going, Death will be awaiting you with a sinister grin on his face."

"Get away from me, you crazy bitch!"

He ignored her like John F. Kennedy ignored the psychics' warning about Dallas. He got into his car and sped away to the house. He looked around and expected to see the Grim reaper waiting for him.

He suddenly saw Omar having violet fur, blue wings, and a long, speared tail rise from the dark wings as the grotesque Creature would from the Black Lagoon.

"Holy hell!" Michael screamed.

"You're gonna find out how holy hell is!" Omar snarled.

The fiendish varmint burst into laughter and zoomed like a rocket into Michael, biting his neck. He screamed bloody murder, disturbing the residents on Amos Mott Road. Sam Mott called the police. Michael was pronounced Dead at the Scene.

Around midnight, David and Cain began wondering where Michael was. Then Joel knocked on the door. Cain answered and heard him say, "Michael's dead."

"How?"

"They found him by that vacant house on Amos Mott Road. They say that he had to have been murdered. By who, they don't know."

"Omar!" David said in a loud whisper.

"Who the hell's Omar?" Joel asked.

"He's one of the demons around there."

"I've heard many stories like that about that place," Joel told him.

"I've been there!" David swore. "Go see for yourself!"

"I will."

Joel left with that. He drove to the house and saw Rachel standing in a black, strapless dress that was above her knees. She was barefoot as well as her long, dark hair was down.

"Excuse me, ma'am. But I'm gonna give you-"

"Joel, you've ten seconds before you blink and hear the bitter cries of death and hell as you begin to drown for eternity in the lake of fire."

He began hearing screeches like a bat. When he saw Omar flying in the air, Joel fired his pistol at him. The demon caught a bullet into his mouth and spat it back at the officer's forehead. Joel bled to death very slowly. Rachel burst into laughter.

It was the next day when Rev. McElven went and poured holy water on the yard. He left after that. Hours later, he died in his sleep. The local newspaper announced that the vacant house was responsible for three deaths in less than twenty-four hours: Rev. Perry McElven, 49; Joel Miles, 29; and Michael McNairy, 18. It also mentioned that Dr.

Raymond E. Prescott, the president of White Mountains Community College, had suspended all classes for two weeks due to the bizarre incidents that'd recently occurred; especially the fact that most of the victims were students there.

He announced over a loudspeaker, "Classes will resume on November the first. Thank you."

The resident halls along with the campus were closed. David was on the way to his car when Naomi asked him, "Where are you gonna stay for two weeks?"

"Maybe at some cheap motel. Gotta be cheap enough to pinch a dime and squeeze snot from Roosevelt's nose."

"You don't have to worry about that."

"Why's that?"

"My parents like you. I think Daddy shouldn't have a problem with you staying at our house."

"That oughta be very nice."

"Well, they're having Gomorrah Falls's autumn carnival all this week."

"Wanna go tonight?"

"Sure."

It was that night when the two were at the carnival and ran into Cain with Rachel in line to the Ferris wheel.

"Cain?" David guessed.

"Rachel?" Naomi guessed.

They both turned around.

"Hello, Naomi," she said.

"David!" Cain said, nodding.

If anyone knew exactly how Rachel got a date with Cain, she'd probably been tied to a stake and burned alive had it been sometime in the Dark Age. She went to the house and waited for the stroke of midnight. Then she took the white sheet of paper on which she'd drew a red heart and wrote CAIN DUONG in it. She burned it after that. She'd cast a love spell on him.

After the carnival, Cain rode with Rachel to the house. After they walked inside, she ordered him to remove his clothes as well as she removed hers. She placed one hand on his chests and the other on his thighs. Suddenly, she pulled him in half like a magician would do to in one of his tricks during his shows.

"David Copperfield, look out! Rachel Rene Mott is behind you!"

"You!" Cain screamed.

"Witch?"

"Burn in hell!"

"That's my line."

Omar came zooming into the window. He swooped Cain up, causing him to scream bloodcurdling screams. David could see a vision of his friend's dreadful death as Ritchie Valens's "La Bamba" was playing on the radio in Naomi's car. She was singing along until he blurted out, "Naomi!"

She turned the radio down.

"What?"

"We gotta go there!"

"Where?"

"The house!"

"What's there for us?"

"Rachel's just put Cain under an evil spell! Now Omar's got him!"

"Holy shit! Who's she think she is? The Bell Witch?"

"All I know is she's not gonna get away with what she just did! That was just purely evil!"

They saw Rachel when they got to the house.

"Hello, David and Naomi."

"I know what you're up to, Rachel," Naomi said.

She drew a pistol at her.

"Pull that trigger if you think you're that brave!"

"You wanna be a witch. You're gonna be burned alive just like one. Except the fire's for eternity! I don't care if you beg for Allah, Jehovah, but He'll have His back turned to you. And Satan's demons will be tormenting you throughout endless nights."

"If I wanna hear preaching, I'll go to church. Now, shoot me if you're gonna do it or put the gun away!"

Naomi fired the pistol and shot Rachel between her eyes. Before she died, she snarled, "I'll get my revenge on you on that night we meet at the fiery gate. Write that in stone, Naomi."

Omar flew up and said, "Hello, David, Naomi."

"Omar," David told him. "Your days are numbered."

"I'll have to see about that!"

Naomi aimed the pistol and fired it between the demon's forehead. She'd loaded the chamber with silver bullets. Therefore, she'd learned that they don't only work on werewolves but demons as well.

DECEMBER

When everyone began to go home from college for the holiday, David announced that he was not going to be returning after he went back to Mississippi. He promised Naomi that they'd keep in touch. On Christmas morning, he got a surprise when he heard Ruth, her mom, answer Naomi's cell phone. She told him that they'd found her dead in her bedroom the night before. He told her that he'd be up there for the funeral. Leah flew with him to New Hampshire. He found out that an angry relative of one victim burned the house to the ground. David had told Leah of the house and said that he had no desire to even go near where it was because the memories of its pure evils would remain with him and the victims' families for life.

THE BITE OF THE BASS

You can be a king or a street sweeper, but
everyone dances with the Grim reaper.
Robert Alton Harris

It was the night of Friday, March 12, 2004, when Alonso and I were at my house and drinking ice-cold Mountain Dew and eating Popeye's fried-chicken as we watched a documentary about vampires' existence on the History Channel. Then he told me, "I know a real vampire-haunted place in Picayune."

"Where's that?"

"Ever heard of 'Ghoulish Games' Cemetery?"

"Isn't that out in Nicholson?"

"Let's go. And I'll show what I'm talking about."

Alonso and I got into his car as he lit a cigarette and told me, "He was this guy named Alvin Bass in the late 1920s. He lived offa Caesar Road and killed bout thirteen people and sucked blood from their bodies. When he was captured, they sent him to the state prison at Parchman. Then they electrocuted his ass in 1931. And the legend has it you can go to his grave at 'Ghoulish Games' Cemetery and walk round it thirteen times. Then you'll feel something bite the hell outta yer neck."

"That's scary," I thought.

Suddenly, we got to the cemetery. I got out and tried to unlatch the gate for both of us. Then I flinched and screamed, "Ow! Dammit!"

"What the hell's wrong with you?" Alonso asked me.

"I burned the hell outta my hand!"

"On that gate?"

"No shit, Plato! I didn't think it'd take such a philosopher to figure that out for himself!"

"Smart ass!" Alonso laughed.

We walked into the cemetery after that and roamed around until we saw a gravestone glowing a sapphire-diamond color.

"That must be it," I told him.

"I am not walking round that gravestone thirteen times, Plax. You can if you want."

On the gravestone, we read:
ALVIN BASS
APR 30 1889
OCT 27 1931
REST IN HELL

I decided to walk around the deranged psychopath's gravestone seven times. Then I heard a voice that I thought to be Alvin Bass telling me, "You've done so well, Plaxton. Don't give up now."

Therefore, I walked around the gravestone six more times and saw that nothing happened.

"Ha!" I laughed.

"What?" Alonso demanded.

"It's only a legend!" I laughed.

Then I felt something bite the hell out of the back of my neck and screamed bloody murder as I fell to the ground. Alonso helped me up and walked me to his car. When he put the key into the ignition, the car wouldn't start.

"Dammit!"

"I guess we'll have to thumb for a ride," I told him.

"I guess you're right."

Then we saw a green truck drive up.

"We're safe!" the both of us thought.

It was my dad!

"What the hell y'all doing gone out to the cemetery this late at night? The law just called and said I had an hour to come pick y'all up or y'all was gone to jail! Get y'all ass in this truck! Now!"

After we climbed into the cab, Dad saw the hideous mark on the back of my neck.

"What the hell's that on the backa yer neck, boy?"

"It's nothing," I lied.

"Boy, don't lie to me. Tell me what that is on the backa yer neck!"

"Lonso and I went out here to check out an urban legend bout a vampire haunting."

"Boy, I've taught you better than that! Yer momma's gonna have a heart attack!"

After that, he turned to Alonso and asked, "Where ya staying tonight, boy?"

"I guess I'll stay with y'all tonight. But I gotta leave tomorrow and get my girlfriend for the dance tomorrow night."

"Sadie Hawkins?"

"Yes, sir."

"Plax, who asked you?" Dad asked me.

I was listening to Janis's lyrics of "Me & Bobby McGee" on the radio as she said, "Freedom was just another word for nothing left to lose."

I told him, "Take it from, Janis."

"That's my boy, Plax," Alonso told me.

When we got to my house, I looked at the mirror in my bedroom and saw the mark on the back of my neck for myself. It was grotesque! I went to bed and tried to not think of the pain. It was at six o'clock the next evening when I was standing in front of the multipurpose building at the high school when Alonso and Heather rode up with his mom.

"Plaxton!" he shouted.

They got out. He asked me, "Plax, you remember Heather?"

"I do. How are you, girl? It's great to see you again!"

"You, too," she told me, smiling.

"Heather, I'd love to dance with you again."

"Sure. I think you're a very lovely dancer, Plaxton."

"I think you are, too. I wasn't born on Rudolph Valentino's birthday for nothing."

"Who was that?"

"He was a romantic actor of the Silent Era-a time that we're too young to remember."

"Plaxton knows bout all them old movies," Alonso declared.

Then he told me, "Well, Plax, we'll see ya inside."

"Alright."

He and I shook hands. I watched him and Heather walk together into the building. I walked into the parking lot and saw Courtney Starkey, an absolutely gorgeous girl, waving to me from her car. I waved back to her, saying, "Hey, girl!"

Then she got out and told me, "Hey, Plaxton."

"How ya doing?" I asked her.

"I'm good. What's that on the backa yer neck?"

"Trust me; you'd rather not know."

"Okay," she laughed.

I walked into the building and paid my admission. I slow-danced with Heather to one slow song. After that, I went outside and talked with a few boys whom I grew up with. There was Michelle McFarland talking along with them.

"Hi, Plaxton," she told me.

"Hey, girl!"

"How are you?"

"I'm good."

Then we heard the deejay playing Kenny Chesney's "You Had Me from Hello." I asked Michelle for a dance. She replied, "Sure, Plax."

She and I walked to the floor and embraced each other. She asked me about my weekend. I told her, "My friend Alonso and I went out to 'Ghoulish Games' Cemetery and checked out the legend about a vampire haunting."

"Oh, did y'all see a vampire?"

"Technically, yeah."

"I was wondering what that was on the backa yer neck. It looks like something bit ya."

"Something actually did."

"Out there?"

"Yes!" I laughed.

"Oh, no."

Suddenly, the song was over. Michelle told me, "Plaxton, it was good to dance with you."

"You, too."

She smiled and walked away. When the dance was over at eleven, word got around about the bite on my neck. Everyone decided to go and have an after party at 'Ghoulish Games' Cemetery. I rode with Alonso, Heather, and another friend out there. At around one am, I ran with several other high-school kids around Alvin Bass's gravestone, taking a dare. After that, we all looked to see young brunette woman standing in a green dress next to the gravestone. Her skin was pale and white. We looked and recognized bloodstains and teeth marks all over her neck. Then she pointed toward the gate and indicated for us to leave immediately!

EXPLANATORY NOTE

First of all, I'd like to explain that none of this happened. However, my friends that appear in this story are based on real people. I just didn't mention them by their real names. That was to protect them of their privacy. The inspiration of this story came to me when I was browsing www.theshadowlands.net/places and found out about a cemetery in Oklahoma. There is a gravestone there having "Mr. Apple" as the inscription. According to legend, you are to walk around the gravestone three times, chanting, "Mr. Apple, are you home?" After that, a bright light will begin chasing you and your neck will have pains. As soon as you get somewhere safe, you'll look at your neck and it'll look as if someone had scratched you so deeply that it left scars. I thought of an idea for a story to write for the anthology that Picayune Writers' Group was sponsoring in 2008 as well as I thought of depraved killers such as Albert Fish and Ed Gein, whose gruesome crimes became inspiration to several slasher-horror movies. That was where Alvin Bass came in. I will be honest with you that there was no such person as serial killer Alvin Bass in Pearl River County, Mississippi, as well as there is no such place as "Ghoulish Games" Cemetery. As Picasso said, I paint objects as I think them, not as I see them.

THE ADVERSARY'S SON

Elizabeth Williams, widow of James G. Williams, Sr., sat alone with her older son of fifteen years by the name of Seth in their three-bedroom apartment in London on the night of October 25, 1967.

"Seth, your brother's been awfully quiet tonight. I wonder what's wrong."

"He's probably pouting over something absolutely pointless."

Nicholas Satan Williams, who was barely twelve, stood alone in the kitchen and listened to his older brother and their mother talk about him. He was also holding a sword that he'd found in a pile of things that James had left behind when he died in May 1964. When Elizabeth was in the middle of a sentence, Nicholas interrupted by screaming at her.

"Mother!"

"Yes, dear," she answered.

"What in the name of all that is pure and holy was going on in your head when you gave me that such cruel name?"

"Son, I don't understand what you're talking about."

"Nicholas Satan Williams! Do you have any bloody idea for whom you named me?"

Elizabeth and Seth sat and thought of ideas for what he was talking about.

"The devil, the father of lies, the adversary! I don't give a damn what you call him!"

Seth became uncomfortable and stood to his younger brother by saying, "Nicholas, you've gone mad. Stop it at once."

"No, Seth. You don't understand that our mother has been cursed of a dangerous mental illness for years. And it is my duty to put her out of her misery once and for all."

Nicholas began running toward Elizabeth with the sword. He shoved Seth out of his way and violently forced the blade into their mother's arm. Elizabeth let out a bloodcurdling scream that disturbed the neighborhood. Nicholas ran outside the apartment as Seth chased him. Local officers watched as he tackled him to the ground and punched his jaw several times.

"What the bloody hell is going on?" an officer demanded.

Neither of the brothers answered. The officer recognized the bloodstains on the blade of the sword that Nicholas was holding.

"Holy Mary, Mother of Jesus!"

"You sick son of the devil!" Seth swore. "You belong in hell. And I'm gonna see that you get there tonight!"

"That's quite enough from both of you!" the officer snapped. "Now, what the bloody hell is going on?"

Elizabeth walked outside the apartment and pointed to Nicholas.

"Get that son of the devil out of my sight!" she screamed.

The officers looked toward Nicholas as one declared, "It's off to the nutshell with you!"

TWELVE YEARS LATER

Nicholas sat alone in his cell at the royal prison for the criminally insane at London shortly after three o'clock on the morning of Thursday, October 25, 1979. Before he could blink his eyes, he saw a mysterious stranger whom appeared to be a younger man in his early twenties and dressed in a black robe and having silver wings, looking like an angel.

"What the bloody hell?" Nicholas wondered as the stranger walked through the three-story window like a ghost.

The stranger didn't say anything at first.

"Who the bloody hell are you?"

"Patience!"

Nicholas sat there and watched as he began to speak.

"Look at yourself, Nicholas Satan."

"Holy bloody hell! Stalker! I say that's what you are!"

"Look around and tell me why you're here, Nicholas."

"It was for my mother's own good! She was horribly sick in her head! And it was my duty to put her out of her misery!"

"It was that cruel name that she had you forsaken by, I know."

"I don't understand what you want!"

"You're anxious to know what news I have for you."

"Yes, I am. Now, tell me what it is that you want of me and be gone about your business!"

"Your father is not who everyone thinks."

"My father James Garfield Williams, Sr., has been dead since May 29, 1964!"

"No!"

"Are you trying to say my mother was unfaithful?"

"Not exactly."

"Then what the bloody hell are you trying to tell me?"

"Your father was the Angel Prince Lucifer of Light millenniums before the Creation. He deceived Eve to eat of the forbidden fruit in the Garden of Eden. He tempted Jesus Christ but miserably failed. And today, he's a menace to all mankind as he roams the earth to rob and murder. The Apostle John speaks of his future when the archangel Michael will chain him to the giant stone inside the bottomless pit in Revelation."

"Tell me no more!" Nicholas screamed, covering his face in shame.

"Had it not been true, I would have told you so. But you are the true begotten son of Satan."

Nicholas looked and listened to him say; "I was what went on in your mother's mind when she named you. Your father sent me to tell you. Your mother, Seth, nor your half-brother James ever knew."

"I have to tell them right away!"

"They're no longer in Britain. Your mother and brother are now current residents in Baltimore, Maryland; in the great nation known as the United States of America."

"You can't be serious!"

The angel nodded and told Nicholas, "Now, it is your mission to go to Baltimore and find them. Tell them of who you are."

Then he held the sword up. Nicholas recognized it as the one that he used to commit the attempted murder of his mother.

"You'll need this as protection. People will know who you are and point you out."

He took the sword and watched the cell door swing widely opened. The clinical assistants couldn't see the angel. They rushed to Nicholas as he ran out the cell. He violently stabbed the three one by one multiple times and ran outside the facility.

"Nicholas Williams!" his psychiatrist Dr. Howard Evans shouted as he stepped out of his car.

"Hello, Dr. Evans!" Nicholas told him, raising the sword.

Dr. Evans was frozen in fear as he watched his patient grin. Nicholas quickly forced the blade into his chest and stabbed him there countless times. After Dr. Evans fell to the damp concrete of the parking lot and died in a puddle of his own blood, Nicholas quickly searched his pockets of his brown coat and took his keys. He jumped into his car and tried to get away. When Nicholas reversed the car, he saw two officers jump in front of him and shouting, "Freeze!"

He ignored them and looked to see a king-sized box of matches in Dr. Evans dashboard and struck one. He put one into his mouth as he stuck his head out the window and exhaled fire onto the officers. Then he sped away at a hundred miles per hour.

When he got to the London Royal Airport, twelve security guards recognized him and ordered him to surrender.

"Didn't your mother ever teach you the polite way to ask?"

"Give it up, Nicholas!" a young officer snapped as he aimed his pistol.

"Apparently not."

Nicholas lit a match and put it to the tip of his tongue. He exhaled fire on the officers and ran. Then he heard, "Final boarding call for Washington, DC."

"Excellent!"

"Where's your pass, sir?" an attendant asked him as he tried to sneak by.

Nicholas snatched him up by his throat and violently slashed his stomach. No one recognized him during the entire flight for Washington, DC. When the plane landed at approximately five PM, a small, elderly woman looked to her middle-aged son and said, "He looks like the young man who escaped the loon house this morning."

Without anyone noticing, Nicholas put a lit match into his mouth and turned to the woman. He exhaled fire into her face and caused her to scream bloody murder.

"That's my mother, you bastard!" her son yelled, trying to swing his fist at Nicholas's face.

He snatched the man's wrist and twisted his arm.

"You're gonna know who my father is," Nicholas snarled.

Then he rushed the blade of the sword into the man's throat. In a matter of seconds, the man was bled to death as well as his mother, who'd recently burned to death. Horrified passengers began screaming as they ran. A young man, who stood at the steps of the plane, pointed and yelled, "That's Nicholas Williams!"

Nicholas violently seized him by his throat and stabbed him in his heart as he pressed down on the sides of his head, crushing his skull.

Everyone was running for his or her lives except for security guards that recognized him. Over the mass chaos, a Washington Police officer shouted through his megaphone, "Nicholas Satan Williams, stop where you are! You're under arrest!"

Nicholas lit a match and exhaled it onto the officers as they ran toward him. He ran until a Washington Patrol car drove in front of him and the officer got on loud speaker, "Stop where you are immediately and put your hands up, Williams!"

Nicholas quickly exhaled fire onto the car, causing it to violently explode and the officer to burn to death in a matter of seconds. He ran through the terminal gate and watched an officer step out of his patrol car. When Nicholas approached the car, the officer drew his revolver and shouted, "Hands on your head, Williams!"

Nicholas pulled his sword at the officer and chopped his hands off. The officer was screaming in horrible pain as he began to stare down at the gun. Nicholas snatched it up and held it at the officer's face as he seized his throat.

"See you in hell, bitch!" he croaked.

Then Nicholas pulled the trigger and sent a bullet through the officer's brain. He jumped into the patrol car and sped away. Seth, who was now twenty-seven, was watching the evening news. An anchorwoman announced, "Today in Britain, Nicholas Satan Williams, a 24-year-old inmate at the royal prison for the criminally insane at London, was reported to escape early this morning. His former psychiatrist Dr. Howard Evans, who diagnosed Williams as paranoid-schizophrenic, was found brutally murdered shortly after.

Also, two security guards were found burned to death in the same area. Only minutes ago, Williams was seen exiting a plane from Britain at Washington National Airport, where he murdered 82-year-old Vestal Gladwell and her 51-year-old Aaron Gladwell, both of Arlington, Virginia. Witnesses proclaim that Williams struck a match and put it into his mouth, then exhaling fire into Mrs. Gladwell's face. After her son attempted to attack Williams, Williams stabbed his throat and caused him to bleed to death. Nicholas is proclaimed to be the mass murderer of over twenty Washington officers before he fled the airport.

Police call him large in armed and extremely dangerous. If anyone sees him, they are to contact the police. Thanks for watching."

Seth turned the TV off and thought, "Dear Mary, Mother of Christ! I have to tell Mother of this!"

He had plans to have dinner with Elizabeth at her house, which was only minutes away from his Baltimore apartment. When he arrived to her house, he couldn't believe who sat and waited for him at the kitchen table. It was his older half-brother James Williams, Jr.

"James, that can't be you!"

James stood from the table and held his arms opened for Seth. He ran and hugged him.

"Just when I thought I'd never see you again!" James declared.

"As terrible as it was over in Vietnam, I'm just glad that you're alive and you're here right now, my brother."

"It was horrible. I was over there for nearly two years."

"But how's your military career now?" Seth asked.

"I'm resigned from the Air Force. I work as a cop in New York."

"And how are Marie and your two daughters Sheila and Valerie?"

"Marie and I finalized for divorce in January. Sorry to say."

"I don't know how to believe it. That girl was madly in love with you."

"But our daughters Sheila, who made six last month, and Valerie, who'll be three next month."

"Tell them that their uncle Seth loves them dearly for me. Will you?"

"I will."

"I will!"

"Aye, Mother," Seth called for Elizabeth.

"Yes, dear."

"What are you cooking?"

"I've ordered a box of Popeye's fried chicken. I cooked mashed potatoes with brown gravy. And I boiled corn on the cob."

"That sounds fantastic!" Seth thought.

"That does for me, too," James said.

She carried a platter of fried chicken toward the table.

"Let me carry that for you, Mother," Seth insisted.

"Thank you, Seth."

James got the silver bowls that contained the mashed potatoes and brown gravy.

"That's one thing that I miss, Liz."

"What's that?"

"Your cooking."

"I have the corn, Mother."

The three sat at the table as they bowed their heads for Seth to pray over the meal.

"Dear Lord, we thank you for another beautifully wonderful day You've given us. We thank You for this food that You've blessed us with. And we ask for You to make us true and thankful with these and all the many blessings. In Your Son Jesus Name, I pray. Amen."

"Let's eat," James insisted.

"James, I think you're very busy as a New York officer."

"I am. I normally stay on duty for twelve hours a day."

"You don't have much time to sleep, do you, James?" Elizabeth guessed.

"Not really," James chuckled.

"I remember going to New York one year," Seth said.

"What did you think of it?" James asked.

"I see why they know it as 'The Greatest City in the World.'"

"I take it you enjoyed it up there."

"It was beautiful!" Elizabeth declared.

"I like Baltimore as well," Seth told James.

"I find a lot of interesting things in Baltimore, too," James said.

"It's where one of America's greatest writers spent most of his time," Seth said.

"Hemingway?"

"Poe."

"I knew that. He's buried here, too, I believe."

"That's correct."

Then Seth looked toward the window and saw Nicholas standing there.

"Nicholas!" he yelled.

Elizabeth and James stared at him, then saw that no one was at the window at all.

"I saw Nicholas at that bloody window!" Seth swore.

"What the bloody hell are you talking about?" Elizabeth demanded.

"Seth, James told him, Nicholas is locked away in an insane asylum in England. For Christ sake, we're in Maryland, which is in the United States of A damn merica!"

"He escaped this morning!"

"You're full of horseshit than a barn house!" James laughed.

"For Christ holy sake! It was all over the evening bloody news!"

Suddenly, a reporter came over the radio, saying:

"At three o' clock this morning, Nicholas Satan Williams, a 24-year-old inmate at the royal prison for the criminally insane at London, escaped."

"I told you so," Seth whispered.

After that, Nicholas drove away to one of Seth's current students by the name of Rene Curtis's house and stalked her at her window. She was on the phone with her boyfriend Robert Tyler.

"Robert, I'm grounded."

"That's bad."

"Did you hear about that nutcase who escaped the asylum in England this morning?"

"What about him?"

"I hear that's Mr. Williams's brother."

"Are you serious?"

"I've heard it."

"You'll find out sooner or later whether if it's the truth or not, Rene," Nicholas snarled.

He jumped from the window before she could see him. He ran to the car and sped away to Westminster Cemetery, which was almost ten miles down the street. He ran to an eighteenth-century crypt and ran down inside it. He had no idea that Baltimore Police were watching him.

"There's Williams!" one officer declared to his partner.

"His ass is grass, and I'm the one who's gonna mow it!"

The two officers ran into the cemetery. One officer pounded on the door of the crypt and shouted, "Nicholas Satan Williams! Get up here with your hands up! NOW!"

Nicholas ran upstairs and forced the blade through the door, stabbing the officer in his chest. The officer screamed like a troop who only thought that he was an atheist until he was in a foxhole.

"Oh, God! Help me!"

The officer screamed as he fell to the ground and died. After that, he stabbed the other officer's heart. Nicholas threw the corpses and hid them inside the crypt.

It was the next morning when Seth stood in front of his first-period class and said, "Good morning, kids."

"Good morning, Mr. Williams."

"Mr. Williams, "Robert blurted out.

"Yes, Robert. And it better be a good one."

"What's this about your brother being an escapee from an asylum in England?"

"How the bloody hell do you know?"

"Word gets around," Robert answered, shrugging his shoulders.

"No! How the bloody hell do you know of my brother?"

"Did you hear of the news last night, Mr. Williams?" Rene asked.

Then Seth jerked his glasses off and covered his face. After that, he walked to his desk and sat down. Despite of all the commotion among his twenty-one students, he shouted, "It's settled! Say no more!"

For one entire minute, the classroom was silent. Seth sighed and said, "Okay, kids. I've decided to give you all a fun day."

"Are we gonna play a game?" Rene asked.

"Very funny, Rene. Actually, what I really had in mind was for you to do whatever as long as you just leave me alone."

"Mr. Williams! You can't be serious!" Robert suggested.

"I'm about as serious as Peter when he denied the Lord at Gethsemane."

"What?" Rene wondered.

"If you read Matthew 26 in the Bible, you'll read of Jesus telling Peter that he'd deny Him for a third time before the old cock's crow. And Peter was very serious about it as well."

"Oh, I get it now!" Rene said.

Seth turned his head from her and began reading Revelation in his Bible. He read to the last verse in Chapter 13. Then the bell rang.

"Class dismissed. Have a blessed day. And I'll see you tomorrow."

Seth's students walked into the hall. After that, he heard a female voice say, "Mr. Seth Williams?"

He looked to see a young, brunette woman, who appeared to be in her early twenties. She was standing in his doorway and stood at five feet and seven inches tall. She wore a white blouse under a brown coat and wore a navy-blue skirt along with black high-heels. Seth stood from his desk and told her, "Good morrow, Miss?"

"I'm Angela Mansfield. I just moved here from Bethel's Hollow, Mississippi. I got my degree in English at Southern Miss in Hattiesburg."

"A Southern girl?"

"Yes, I am!"

"How marvelous it is to meet you, Ms. Mansfield!"

"You don't have to call me Ms. Mansfield. I'm just Angela. I'm filling in for Mr. Lambert, who's retiring next month."

"Mr. Thomas Lambert?"

"Yes."

"He was such a marvelous teacher. I'm gonna hate to see him go."

"Well, he told me some things about you."

"He didn't tell you anything bad of me, did he?"

"He told me that you came over here from England."

"That's correct. Can't you tell by my accent?"

"I hear it. So, what do you teach, Mr. Williams?"

"I teach English and world literature. Listen, Angela. I don't mean to be impolite by questioning your age, but-"

"I'm twenty-three. And I don't mind."

"I'm only twenty-seven. So, I'll answer to Seth for you."

"Okay," Angela laughed.

"English is a very important thing to have, Angela."

"It is, Seth. I agree."

"Next week, we begin midterms. I'm having my students study Romeo & Juliet by William Shakespeare and The Picture of Dorian Gray by Oscar Wilde."

"I never could stand Shakespeare's works. I always enjoyed works by Edgar Allan Poe."

"'The Raven!'"

"That was my favorite of his. And I liked his horror tale 'The Fall of the House of Usher.'"

Then the bell rang for second-period class. Angela smiled and told him, "It was very wonderful to meet you, Seth. Hopefully, we'll see each other again, soon."

"It shouldn't be that long."

"I hope you have a wonderful day."

"I hope you'll do the same, Angela."

"Thank you."

It was that evening at around seven when Seth sat alone in his one-bedroom apartment and looked for Angela's number in a phonebook. He dialed the number and heard her answer the second ring.

"Hello."

"Good evening, Angela."

She didn't recognize his voice and told him, "Listen, if you're wanting to sell something, thank you very much. But I'm not interested."

" This is Seth!"

She was surprised by his call.

"I found your number in the phonebook and thought of giving you a call. I hope you don't mind."

"Actually, I don't mind at all. What's going on?"

"I was wondering, Angela."

"Yes."

"Do you like Mexican food?"

"I love Mexican food!"

"That's fantastic!"

"To be honest, I wanted to know if you'd like to do anything for dinner this evening. Maybe if you don't wanna go alone."

"Seth, I don't think that'll be a good idea."

"Well, I apologize for bothering."

"Don't apologize!"

"Why the bloody hell shouldn't I?"

"Actually, I think it'd be a wonderful idea for me to have dinner with you tonight, Seth!"

"You can't be serious!"

"You better believe so."

"Where would you like to go?"

"I'd like to try that Mexican place called Alberto's."

"That is fantastic! I'll pick you up at eight."

"Sounds great, Seth."

"I will see you then, Angela."

"Bye, Seth."

At Alberto's, a young, Hispanic waiter by the name of Carlos walked up and told them, "Good evening. I'll be your server. What may I get for you to drink?"

"I'd like a margarita," Seth answered.

"And for you, Senorita?"

"I'd like a Pepsi-Cola."

"Muchos Gracias."

When Carlos walked back into the kitchen, Seth lit up a cigarette and flicked the ashes into a small ashtray.

"Would you like a cigarette, Angela?"

"No, thanks, Seth. I don't smoke."

Suddenly, he recognized Nicholas walk inside the restaurant. He had his long, black hair covering his face when an hombre told him, "Good evening, Senora."

Nicholas pulled his hair back and asked, "Do I look like a blood Senora to you?"

"You must pardon me, Senora. It was the long hair."

"You're gonna find out whether if I'm a Senor or Senora very shortly. I guarantee it."

"Please don't hurt me!"

Nicholas jerked the hombre by the sides of his head and caused him to scream as he could feel his skull cracking. The other employees began staring in horror as they watched Nicholas lift him up and toss him into the double-door of the kitchen. The hombre's corpse landed into a frying-hot pan and caught on fire. The crew ran from the fire. Nicholas lit a match, put it into his mouth, and exhaled fire onto them as they tried to run passed him.

"Angela! We gotta get outta here!"

Seth jumped from the table. He and Angela ran along with the other horrified customers outside the restaurant without Nicholas seeing them. Suddenly, a fire truck drove into the driveway of Alberto's. Nicholas ran behind hit and exhaled fire onto it. The truck exploded, killing the firefighters.

"See ya in hell, Nicholas Satan Williams!" Carlos yelled behind him.

Nicholas turned to see him having his middle finger up. The waiter began running as he walked toward him. He jumped into his car and gave Nicholas another bird. Then Nicholas lit a match and put it into his mouth. He exhaled fire onto the car and caused it to explode, killing the waiter.

"I loved that restaurant," Seth regretted.

"I'm sorry," Angela told him.

"That was my brother."

"Your brother is Nicholas Satan Williams?"

Seth nodded his head and replied, "Yes."

"I can't believe that."

"Believe it because it's the truth."

Seth drove to Baltimore Apartments, where Angela was living, and walked her to her door.

"Have a good night, Seth."

"You do the same, Angela."

"See ya tomorrow."

On the late local news, a Baltimore anchorwoman stood in front of the remains of Alberto's and said, "Earlier this evening, Nicholas Williams was spotted here at Alberto's. Williams was reported to have walked inside the restaurant and murdered 32-year-old employee Eduardo Sanchez. Also 26-year-old Carlos Gonzalez was found burned to death inside his vehicle afterward. At the exact time that Nicholas committed this horrible crime, his older brother Seth Williams was said to have been seen at the restaurant. There's no information about where either of the Williams brothers are at this time."

Seth turned the TV off and heard his neighbor Mrs. Marie Goldfield screaming. He jumped up and ran to her two-bedroom apartment. When he swung her door opened, she screamed, "Your brother!"

"Oh, dear to Jesus!"

"Why didn't you kill that evil bastard for yourself when you took the knife from your mother's arm? It sure would a solved a lotta today's problems!"

"Mrs. Goldfield, I hope you're not questioning my business. I know you wouldn't think it'd be polite for me to question yours."

"I'm sorry, Seth!"

"For Christ sake, where the bloody hell is that granddaughter of yours?"

"Lori's out with her fiancé."

"The cops are running all over Baltimore tonight, looking for some evil bastard!" Seth complained, pulling his glasses off.

"Of course."

"What the hell is Lori doing out when she should be at home, tending to her 86-year-old grandmother?"

Then he stepped outside and watched twenty patrol cars drive by. Nicholas, who was standing on the rooftop of the apartment complex, exhaled fire from the match that was lit inside his mouth. The fire struck the cars, causing them to explode like a line of dominos falling. Other patrol cars began speeding up. Finally, a car managed to drive into Mrs. Goldfield's driveway. When Lori got out with her fiancé, Seth ran to her and demanded, "Lori, what the bloody hell are you doing out on a night like this when you got your grandmother to look after?"

"What are you doing over here, Seth?" she demanded.

"You better mind your own business before I bitchslap you all the way to London!" her fiancé snapped.

"Don't be cocky with me, mister! I'm not in the bloody mood!"

"You two, cut it out," Lori told them.

"I'm sorry, Lori," Seth told her.

"Gilbert, this is our neighbor Seth Williams," Lori said to her fiancé.

"How do you do, Gilbert?"

"As you can probably tell, Seth was raised in England. That's their way of saying 'How's it going?'"

"I'm doing quite alright, Seth," he answered, shaking his hand.

"Good for you. For me, I need to go home."

"Have a good night, Seth," Lori told him.

"Bye, Lori," he sighed.

When he got back to his apartment, he heard his phone ringing. He quickly ran inside and answered it.

"Hello!"

"How's it going, Seth?"

"James?"

"Yes, it is."

"Well, James, I wish I could say that I was doing as well as you probably are at this time."

"What's wrong?"

"You'd rather not know."

"Okay. Well, I thought it'd be great for us two brothers to take a ride together."

"Jimmy, why do you wanna go out on a night like this?"

"Well, we hadn't done it since November 1975. That's been nearly four years."

"I just had my 86-year-old neighbor brutally attacked by our brother. You know, the one whom we don't claim at all."

"I do know who you're talking about."

"And what else was horrible was her 23-year-old granddaughter was out with her fiancé who she's marrying shortly after Christmas this year and had left her alone. I thought it was a crying shame."

"Seth, please calm down."

"There were at least fifty Baltimore cops burned to death in a mass killing tonight as well."

"How the hell did that happen?"

"Seth, I'll be over there in a few minutes."

"No, Jim!"

"Why on Earth not?"

"Maybe tomorrow night."

"That's just dandy for me."

"Goodnight, Jimmy."

"Goodnight to you as well, Seth."

The next day was Saturday, October 27, 1979. Seth woke up by the phone ringing at around eight in the morning. He answered the second ring by saying, "Hello."

"Good morning, Seth."

"Hello, Angela."

"I was wondering if you'd like to join me for breakfast at Krispy Kreme for coffee and donuts."

"I'd love to!"

"I'll be waiting for you."

When he arrived to the donut shop, he saw Angela sitting at a table by the window. She smiled and waved to him. He nodded to her and walked inside the door. Then he recognized the blond who was sitting next to her.

"Seth, this is my friend Denise."

"It's very nice to meet you, Denise."

"Very nice to meet you as well, Seth. Would you like to sit down?"

"I'd love to. Thank you very much!"

"You're very welcomed."

He sat down and pulled a fudge-glazed donut from the box in the center of the table.

"Would you like some coffee, Seth?" Angela asked.

"That'd be great. Thank you."

She poured a small cup of coffee for him. Then he asked Denise, "How did you and Angela meet?"

"We're neighbors."

Then he quoted Fred Rogers by saying, "It's a beautiful day in the neighborhood."

Angela and she laughed until she said, ""Seth, I hear Nicholas Williams, the serial killer on the loose in Baltimore, is your brother."

Seth spat out his coffee and demanded, "What did you just ask me?"

"Why did he end up in the prison for the criminally insane to begin with?" Denise asked him.

"His full name is Nicholas Satan Williams."

"That's why he tried to kill your mother?"

"Yes!"

"I also hear a rumor that he proclaims to be the true begotten son of Satan."

"I wouldn't know."

Then he changed the subject by telling Angela, "My student Rene Curtis is having a party at her house next weekend."

"Do you wanna go?" Angela asked him.

"I'm thinking of it."

"I'll probably go with you if you go at all."

It was that morning when Robert was woken by the phone.

"Hello," he answered.

"What are you doing, boy?"

"I was asleep until you called."

"That sounds like fun."

"Rene, I'm glad you called because I have a question to ask you."

"What's that?"

"Are you a virgin?"

"Yes, but I'm only fourteen."

"You can lose it tonight."

"I don't know about that, Robert."

"Well, I'll talk to you later, sweetie."

"Bye."

Rene lied in her bed. Then she heard Nicholas call her name.

"Who are you?"

When she looked, she saw no one at the window.

"Close your eyes and count to ten. Once you open, I'll be there."

She closed her eyes and counted to ten. She opened her eyes and saw him standing there. She screamed, then turned her back to him and pulled her shorts to her ankles. Nicholas began walking backward until he fell out of the window. He stared out of her buttocks sticking out of the window and shouted, "I'm gonna get that big booty!"

She pulled her shorts back to her waist and watched him stand up.

"I'll be back for you at eleven tonight! Prepare to die, Rene Elizabeth Curtis!"

Rene dialed Seth's number and heard him answer the second ring.

"Hello."

"Mr. Williams?"

"Who's calling?"

"This is Rene Curtis."

"Hello, Rene. How may I help you?"

"Actually, I met your brother just now."

"James?"

"The other one."

"Holy shit! You can't be serious!"

"I am."

"Where are you?"

"I'm at my house."

"I was just making sure that you were okay."

"I'm doing fine."

"Great. Hopefully, I'll see you tonight."

It was that evening when Seth heard his phone ringing. He answered the second ring and heard James say, "How's it going, Seth?"

"Not as well as I had planned," he sighed.

"What the hell's going on?"

"Nicholas assaulted one of my students this morning."

"Really?"

"Yes!"

"Well, do you still wanna go for a ride?"

"Sure, Jimmy. I'd love to."

When James arrived at Seth's apartment, Seth went to his car and got into the front seat. Seth put a cigarette to his mouth and lit it.

"I didn't know you were a smoker."

"I am."

"Since when?"

"Three years in January."

"How long has it been since you drank?"

"Last night was the first time since your bachelor party."

"That's been at least eight years."

"I've never suffered alcoholism. That's one good thing."

"I guess you could say that."

Seth tossed the cigarette out the window. James snapped, "I write people fines for that in New York!"

"This is bloody Baltimore in the bloody State of Maryland!"

"I never liked a litterbug, Seth. Just like I tell people up there; I'm not your momma, so it's not place to pick up after you."

"I won't do it any more."

"Thanks."

"How do you like your job in New York?"

James sighed and told him, "Well, earlier this year, I was a pallbearer for a cop who was shot to death for money in his wallet."

"That's sad."

"What's even sadder is his murderer was a fifteen-year-old boy."

"What did they give him for a penalty?"

"He's going up for trial in March."

Suddenly, James made it to a small bridge where he and Seth saw Nicholas standing. Needless to say, he knew that his brothers were going to pass through there and already had a match lit inside his mouth. When he exhaled the fire, James swerved his car to avoid it. He ended up driving the car off the bridge. He and Seth jumped from the car as quickly as they could.

"It's gonna be a long way back to New York," James said as he watched the car fall into the stream below the bridge.

"A very long way," Seth added.

The two saw that Nicholas was gone.

"We better go tell someone," James suggested.

They walked up the road until they saw a small café. They walked inside and saw a blond, young woman standing at the counter.

"I'm also hungry," James whispered to Seth.

"Good evening, gentlemen," the girl told them.

"Good evening," Seth told her.

"What may I get for you boys?"

""Do you have T-bone steak?" James asked.

"Yes. How would you like that cooked?"

"Medium-rare, please."

"You got it. What may I get for you to drink?"

"I'd like a Pepsi-Cola."

She looked at Seth and heard him say, "I'd like a hamburger steak, please."

"What would you like for your side orders?"

"French fries and mashed potatoes with brown gravy."

"What may I get for you to drink?"

"Barq's root beer."

"Yes, sir."

A minute later, the waitress was back with their beverages and told them, "I should have your meals out in about ten minutes."

"No problem," James told her.

Several minutes later, she was back with their meals. James opened the A-1 bottle and got a huge surprise!

"Holy shit! It's blood!"

"You might wanna tell someone about that," Seth told him when he buried his spoon into his scoop of mashed potatoes with brown gravy.

Then he realized that he scooped up a live tarantula.

"Holy, bloody hell!" he screamed, jumping from his chair.

When he looked out the window, he saw Nicholas standing there.

"It's Nicholas!" he yelled. "Call the police!"

"And look what he's got!" James yelled when he saw Nicholas holding a rifle.

He fired through the window and watched the bullet strike the waitress in the back of her head. All the employees and customers watched her decapitated corpse fall to the floor. They were vomiting as they ran from the restaurant. James and Seth ran outside the café and caught a taxi.

Meanwhile, Robert got off his bicycle at Rene's house and rang her doorbell.

"I'm coming!" she shouted, running to the door.

When she answered, he asked, "Are you ready?"

"I was born ready!"

"That's what I'd like to hear."

When they got to her room, she began stripping. When she was completely naked, she looked at Robert and snapped, "Get naked for Christ sake!"

Robert stripped down and ran to her bed.

"I gotta use the bathroom right quick!" he told her.

"Hurry back!"

While Robert was using the bathroom, Nicholas caught Rene with her eyes closed and sneaked through her window. He poured a line of glue onto her stomach and hurried back out of her window. Robert walked back into the room and lied on top of her.

Hour later, Robert looked at his wristwatch and saw that it was after eleven.

"Rene!"

"What?"

"It's almost midnight! I gotta get home!"

When he tried to stand up, he noticed that he was glued to her.

"What the hell?" Rene wondered.

Nicholas opened the window and burst into laughter.

"I should a known it was you, Nicholas Satan Williams!" Rene told him.

"I was wanting to do you two a favor. You wanted to be together forever. Be careful what you wish for; it might not be exactly what you expected."

Robert broke loose from Rene and put his underwear on.

"You sick bastard!"

When he began running toward him, Nicholas jumped out of the window.

"Nicholas Williams is a little bitch!" Robert shouted.

Then he kissed Rene and told her, "Bye, baby."

"Bye."

He put the rest of his clothes on and rode home. Rene lied down on her bed and turned the radio on.

"Just this evening at the Old Baltimore Café, Nicholas Williams was seen as well as his older brothers James Williams of New York City and Seth of Baltimore. The both of them proclaim that Nicholas pulled a sickeningly sadistic prank on both of them. That was when Nicholas fired a thirty-thirty rifle through the window and decapitated waitress Barbara Marie Anderson, a 24-year-old native of Baltimore."

Rene turned the radio off, then heard her dad walk into the room.

"Daddy!"

"Hello, Princess."

"How was work?"

"The usual. Twelve hours of exhaustion. But it pays our bills. So it's worth it."

"Well, welcome home, Daddy."

She stood up and kissed his cheek.

"I love you, Daddy," she whispered.

"I love you as well, Princess."

After that, Nicholas drove to Baltimore Apartments. He covered his face and walked to where Angela lived. He found out that she wasn't home. Therefore, he stalked Denise, who was taking a shower. After several minutes in the shower, she saw Nicholas appear through the shower door.

"What the hell are you doing?"

Then Nicholas poked the glass in the shower door and shattered it. No one heard Denise's screams as he stabbed her countless times. She fell forward and got severely cut by the sharp glass. She was lying there cold, wet, and naked as she heavily bled.

He lit a match and put it to his mouth. Then he exhaled the fire onto her, causing her corpse to burn. Minutes later, the other residents were awaken by the disturbing smell of Denise's corpse burning.

The next morning was Sunday, October 28, when Seth watched the news about Denise's murder. He called Angela and was glad when she answered the second ring by saying, "Hello."

"Angela! Thank God!"

"Seth, I'm so happy!"

"I heard the news! They identified that corpse as Denise!"

"I know."

Angela began weeping. Then Seth told her, "Angela, I'd like for you to meet my mother and my half-brother."

"I'd love to."

"Well, I'll see you at approximately twelve o'clock."

"That'll be good."

He hung up and waited for nearly two hours. He drove to get Angela from Baltimore Apartments.

"Seth!" she cried.

He had a red rose for her.

"Is that for me?"

"Indeed, it is."

"That's so sweet, Seth! May I have a hug?"

"Certainly."

Seth embraced her gently and asked her, "Are you ready to go to lunch?"

"Absolutely."

"Let's go."

At the table at Elizabeth's kitchen, James asked Angela, "Where are you from, Angela?"

"I'm from Mississippi. It's a big city that most people have never heard of."

"I've never been there," Elizabeth told her.

"Neither have I," James said.

"Where are you from? I can tell that you're not from England."

"I was raised in New York."

"I was wondering why you don't sound like Liz and Seth."

"Actually, Seth and I aren't full brothers. Our father was married for his first time in 1943. That was my mother. Then our father James Williams, Sr., went back to England when I was about eight months old and ended up and abandoning my mother and me. That's how he met Liz. And when he married Liz, she was seven months pregnant with Nicholas. Seth was three at the time. I was just days shy of my sixth birthday."

"That's an interesting story," Angela told him.

"What's also interesting is James and I didn't meet each other until I was five and he was eight," Seth told her.

"I bet it was scary for both of you," Angela thought.

"It was," James told her. "Because the both of us were too young to understand anything like that."

Later on, Seth told Elizabeth and James, "Mother, Jim, it's been a great evening. But Angela and I are going, now."

It was approximately nine that night when Nicholas sneaked down to Washington and managed his way into the basement of an elderly couple's three-story house. The couple's small great-grandson walked down there and looked around after he heard Nicholas move inside the closet.

"Mickey," Nicholas whispered.

"Who's there?"

"I'm the monster living in the closet."

The boy became frightened and ran upstairs, shouting, "Grandpa! Grandma! There's a monster in the basement!"

"Mick, what the devil are you trying to say?" the old man demanded.

"I heard a bad man in the closet down in the basement!"

He tugged his grandfather's wrist and led him downstairs to the basement.

"Hello!" the man yelled.

It was dead silent until the man repeated, "Hello!"

Nicholas still didn't answer his call.

"Okay, whoever you are; the joke's over. If you don't show yourself in ten seconds, I'm calling the police."

Nicholas still refused to answer. Then the man looked to his grandson and asked him, "Have I ever told you about the shepherd boy who cried wolf?"

The boy nodded no.

While they were walking upstairs, the man sighed and told the boy, "The shepherd boy was tending to his flock of sheep alone one day and began shouting 'Wolf!' The townspeople became worried and ran to see what his problem was. He laughed when he realized that he'd fooled them. And he cried wolf for a second time. They came for him again. He laughed at how he fooled them again. The third time, a wolf was attacking him. He cried wolf. But no one came to help him. Then the wolf killed the boy and his sheep."

The boy shrugged his shoulders and asked, "Why are you telling me this, Grandpa?"

"What I wanted to tell you is you can't trust a liar even when he tells the truth."

"I understand."

"That was quite an interesting story, Grandpa," Nicholas said as he jumped behind them.

The man and the boy quickly turned around. Nicholas grabbed his sword and stabbed the man in his stomach. The boy ran upstairs, screaming, "Grandma!"

The man's wife turned the TV off and demanded, "My heavens! What in the world is wrong with you, Michael?"

"There was this bad man who just killed Grandpa in the basement!"

"I think you just had a nightmare, son. That's all."

Then Nicholas threw the old man's bloody corpse at her and said, "Believing comes from seeing, bitch!"

The woman was screaming as she jumped back. Then she looked to her shelf above her shelf and grabbed the crucifix that was sitting next to her Bible and held it toward Nicholas.

"Who the hell do you think I am? Dracula?"

He put a lit match into his mouth and exhaled fire on the woman's fist. She dropped the crucifix as she screamed, "I'm burning!"

Nicholas watched the boy run toward the phone and knew that he was planning to dial 9-1-1. Therefore, he jumped in his way and chopped the chord from the phone.

"Who you gonna call now?"

"Someone help me!" the woman screamed as she began to burn worse.

Nicholas turned to the refrigerator and opened it to find a bottle of Jack Daniels. He pulled the bottle out and ran to the woman, pouring it all over her burning arm. She caught on fire as he stabbed her heart. After she fell to the floor and died, Nicholas turned to the boy and told him, "Run, little Mickey! Whatever you do, don't look back! That is, of course, unless you wanna end up like Lot's wife: a pillar of salt!"

Nicholas burst into laughter and watched the boy run from the house. After the boy was completely out of sight, Nicholas drove to David Marlowe, Sr.'s house and peeked through the front window to see the small twin brothers whom Rene was babysitting. They were watching Frankenstein on TV. She was on the phone while ordering pizza from Pizza Hut. After she got off the phone, she saw the scene in which the monster threw the child into the pond and watched her drown.

"You two, getting scared?"

The boys nodded no.

"Good. Because there is no bogeyman or Frankenstein. You understand?"

The boys nodded yes.

"You two are so smart."

An hour later, Rene tucked the twins into bed as she read "The Raven" by Edgar Allan Poe. Then one of the twins saw Nicholas appear at the window.

"There he is!" one twin cried.

Rene turned and saw him.

"Go! Run and hide! Find a closet! I don't care where! Just go where he can't see you!"

The boys obeyed Rene and ran from their bedrooms. Rene ran to the boys' bedroom and grabbed their dad's rifle. When she turned around, she saw Nicholas at the doorway.

"Put that gun down, bitch!" he snarled.

"Give me just one second."

After the rifle went off, the bullet struck Nicholas's chest. He fell to the floor and lied facedown. Rene ran and found the boys in the closet in the bathroom.

"Babies!"

She was so happy to see them as they jumped into her lap.

"Is he gone?" one asked.

Rene nodded and said, "Yes, he's dead."

"You killed the bogeyman?"

"Listen to me, you two. Go down to Mrs. Lewis's house and knock on her door. When she answers, I want you to ask her to call the police and have them come here."

After she watched the two boys run outside their front door, Rene went back to their parents' bedroom and Nicholas was gone.

"What the hell?" she wondered.

Minutes later, the police pounded on the front door.

"I'll be there in a moment!" Rene told them.

She hurried to the door and answered.

"We just got a call from Margaret Lewis that there was trouble at this residence," the officer told her.

"Actually, yes!"

"Apparently, we're here to arrest someone for armed burglary. Am I correct?"

"Actually, it was Nicholas Williams, believe it or not. I shot him dead."

She showed them the rifle and swore, "I shot him in this room! Honest!"

The officers flashed their flashlights on the floor and didn't see any bloodstains or any marks where Nicholas fell. Then Col. Jones looked to her and snapped, "Wipe that damn smile off your face!"

"I'm not smiling."

"You think this is funny?"

"I shot him in this room and watched him die in that floor!"

"Gentlemen, we gotta go. We don't even have time for this bullshit!"

"What bullshit?" Rene demanded.

"Don't do this again. Or we'll have you arrested. Unless you can afford to pay a $1000 fine."

After the officers left the house, Rene dialed Robert's number and heard his dad answer the third ring.

"Hello."

"Hi, is Robert home by chance?"

"Actually, he is. Just one second."

"Hello."

"Robert, you won't believe this."

"What, babe?"

"I just killed Nicholas Williams!"

"What the hell are you talking about?"

"The police don't know how to believe me. I shot him to death with David Marlowe's pistol while I was babysitting his twin sons David and Daniel. Then I told them to go to the neighbor's house and have her call the police. When they got there, Nicholas's body was gone.

There were no bloodstains or any prints where he fell in that room. I thought it was so weird!"

"That is weird," Robert thought.

"Robbie, believe me!"

"I will," he sighed. "Thanks," she told him.

"You're welcome. And I'll come over in a few minutes. Stay put."

Several minutes later, Robert drove up in his dad's Pontiac. As David and Daniel ran out there to see him, they shouted, "Robert!"

"Hey, kids!"

He walked inside the house and kissed Rene's lips. Then he turned to David and Daniel and asked them, "You boys wanna go get ice-cream?"

"Yay!"

"Let's go!"

Then he turned to Rene and asked, "Can you come with me?"

"I'd love to, Robbie."

In the car, he pulled a cold bottle of Budweiser from his seat and gave it to Rene. He put a cigarette to his mouth and lit it. When he got to the store, he ran inside and got two Flintstones ice cream bars. Then he ran back to the car and gave them to the boys.

"Thank you, Robbie!"

"You're welcomed."

Robert put the car in gear and drove back to the Marlowes' house. David, Sr. was sitting with his wife Rebecca in her car as they waited for them. Both Robert and Rene felt their heart skip a beat when they saw looks of fury on their faces.

"Holy shit!" Rene thought, jumping from the car.

"I gotta go!" Robert told her.

After he let David and Daniel out of his car, he sped away. Rene walked up to their parents.

"Where were you?" Rebecca demanded.

"Mommy, Rene's boyfriend took us to get ice-cream," Daniel told her.

Rebecca didn't tell him anything. David, Sr., looked at Rene and demanded, "Why were you playing with my guns, young lady?"

She rolled her eyes and said, "No one believes me!"

"About what?" he demanded.

"I shot the serial killer who's got everyone talking."

Then her dad drove up. She ran and climbed into the cab.

"Young lady!"

"Yes, Daddy."

"What the hell are you doing, playing with guns? Don't you know you could get someone severely injured like that?"

"How the hell do you know?"

"The police called me and your mother about it. They said you tried to convince them you shot and killed Nicholas Williams."

"I shot him, Daddy. And I watched him die."

"Have you been drinking? I smell it on your breath?"

"I only drank one with Robert this evening."

"What were you doing with Robert while you were supposed to be tending to two four-year-old boys?"

"I called him to tell him about what happened. He came over to see if we were alright."

"You're grounded, young lady. You got me? For a month!"

BOSTON

Nicholas jumped a midnight train for Boston and hid very well. None of the passengers recognized him during the entire-six hour ride. When he exited the train, he had his long hair over his face and walked away as people stared at him.

"Who's that man, Mommy?" a little boy asked.

"I don't know. But he sure is weird."

Nicholas pulled his hair back and demanded, "Do you recognize me, now?"

Numerous people stared in horror as he pulled his sword and beheaded the woman's husband. The woman and little boy ran. Then a security guard watched Nicholas run as he shouted, "Freeze!"

He put a lit match into his mouth and turned to the officer, then exhaled fire into his face. The security guard screamed as he was on fire and jumping around. Nicholas ran until he saw a Holiday Inn. There, he saw a young woman, no older than twenty, at the pool.

"Don't you wanna go for a swim?" she asked the boy who was with her.

She had a Southern accent. Therefore, Nicholas could tell that she was a guest at the hotel. She told the boy, "This shouldn't be could for y'all Yankees here in Massachusetts."

"Where are you from anyway?"

"Auburn, Alabama."

When she took her robe off, she was completely naked and the boy told her, "You're crazy."

"You're chicken!"

Then she jumped into the pool. The boy laughed and said, "I bet you're freezing your ass off in that water!"

The boy looked to Nicholas and said, "Excuse me, sir. This pool is for registered guests only."

Nicholas pulled his hair back and walked through the gate and asked, "How would you like to take a permanent vacation?"

"Are you trying to offer me tickets to Disney World?"

Nicholas laughed and said, "That's a great guess. But not even close."

"Well, where?"

"In fact, I was wanting to take you to the South and let you thaw out for a while. After all, eternity is quite a while."

"Get the hell away from me, you freak!"

"Apparently, we haven't been introduced."

"Fortunately not."

"I hear the opposite of what people tell me. I hear that you don't want me to bring hell to you. So, I'll bring you to hell!"

Nicholas grabbed the sword and seized the sword. He stabbed his heart and carved to his navel.

The boy screamed until he died. The girl ran as Nicholas tried to throw the boy's corpse at her. It landed in the pool. He ran to catch the girl running inside the lobby, screaming, "Y'all gotta help me!"

They all stared at her as if they thought that she'd only went crazy until Nicholas forced the sword's blade into her back. The girl screamed until Nicholas pulled the blade out. Then he pulled a stake from his pocket and hammered it into the top of her head. She was finally dead after that. Everyone stared until he screamed, "What the hell are you all staring at?"

Then he put a lit match into his mouth and exhaled fire all over the lobby. Everyone ran for his or her lives after that.

BALTIMORE

Seth was watching the news when he heard the reporter say, "What numerous people of Baltimore thought of Nicholas Williams was sadly incorrect. He is alive and well. Massachusetts State Police reported to have seen him in Boston, where he brutally massacred two people, ages nineteen and twenty-two, at the pool at a Holiday Inn last night. Then he killed over twenty people in the lobby. Williams remains at large in both at armed and extremely dangerous. Baltimore Police are still on search for him."

Seth turned the TV off and swore, "The evil bastard won't be alive once I see him again!"

He picked up the pistol that was lying on his sofa, then heard Nicholas jump from the ceiling. He became hopeless when he found that the chamber was completely empty after he attempted to fire at Nicholas.

"Shit!"

Nicholas forced a napkin that was covered in bull turds into Seth's face.

"It was a gift of brotherly love from me to you. From a bull's ass to your face."

Seth didn't say anything. He ran to his bedroom and looked for bullets in the top drawer under his bedstead. After he didn't find any, he thought, "Apparently, there's been a thief in my house."

When he ran out of his room, he saw that Nicholas was gone and thought, "Better run!"

He looked at the clock and read 7:52 a.m. and remembered that he had to take James to the airport like he'd promised. He sped to the McHenry Inn and got James, who'd just checked out. At the airport, he told Seth, "Your mother has my number. You're welcomed to call me at any time."

"I'm gonna miss you, Jimmy."

"I'm gonna miss you."

The brothers hugged each other. Seth cried as he watched James walk through the gate. Then he went to the school. He saw Angela.

"Hi, Seth."

"Hi, Angela."

"Why are you so sad?"

"James just went back to New York."

"I'm sorry to hear that."

"It happens."

"Would you like to join me at Benito's for lunch? I hear it's very good."

"I'd love to!"

Then Robert and Rene interrupted them.

"Mr. Williams!" Rene said.

"Yes, Rene."

"Did you hear?"

"Did I hear what?"

"I'm not such a hero after all."

"I heard," Seth sighed.

"What's she talking about?" Angela demanded.

"Nicholas killed about forty people in Massachusetts last night," Seth answered.

"What?"

Angela was curious.

"But does that mean your party's canceled for this weekend?" Seth asked.

FRIDAY, NOVEMBER 2, 1979

Seth picked Angela up from her apartment and asked, "Ready to have a helluva night?"

"Am I, now?"

"That's my girl!"

Then Angela heard Janis Joplin singing "Maybe" on Seth's radio and turned the volume up.

"I love this song, Seth!"

"Really?"

"Yes! I slow-danced to it with my high-school sweetie at our Homecoming in our senior year."

"Didn't you say you were twenty-three?"

"Yeah. I graduated in 1974. Janis was dead three years before that."

"I was just ending my sophomore year at Hopkins. I was twenty-two."

"How long have you been a teacher, Seth?"

"I began in September of this year."

"How do you like it?"

" I love it. I plan to retire in 2012. That's going to be a long time from now."

"It certainly is."

"I plan to earn my Ph.D. in educational administration as well."

"When are you gonna do that?"

"Who knows?"

Then he drove into Rene's driveway and watched dozens of teens running in her front yard.

"Mr. Williams!" one shouted.

"What's going on?"

"Not much. Well, not for now."

When Seth and Angela walked inside, Rene greeted them.

"Mr. Williams! Ms. Mansfield! I'm so glad you guys could come!"

"So are we," Seth declared.

"How old are you?" Seth asked her.

"Fourteen."

"I'm almost twice your senior. I'll be twenty-eight on March 27, 1980."

"You two want a beer?" Robert asked.

"No, thanks," Angela laughed.

After a while, two boys sat on Rene's doorstep when Nicholas walked up. He had his long hair over his face.

"Holy shit! It's Nicholas Williams!" one boy shouted.

The other boy got his camera out and tried to take a photo of him. Nicholas snatched it from his hand and demanded, "Whatcha gonna take a photo of now, Larry?"

He pulled the sword out and stabbed Larry's heart until he died. Ricky, his friend, ran to the basement and alerted everyone.

"Everyone! Nicholas Williams is here!"

The music was stopped as everyone laughed.

"He just killed Ricky!"

Then Nicholas crept behind him and said, "He speaks the truth!"

"Holy bloody hell!" Seth snapped.

"Don't do it, Seth!" Angela told him.

"I got this, Angela!"

Seth stood there until Nicholas told him, "Don't do everything that bitch tells you."

Then Robert thought, "I'm damn sure glad I got my gun!"

"Robbie! Don't!" Rene begged.

145

"It's okay, babe."

Nicholas laughed and said, "You don't even have the heart!"

"Oh, yeah?"

"Yeah!"

Nicholas put a lit match on his tongue as Robert told him, "I got a bullet in this chamber having 'Reserved for Nicholas Satan Williams' printed on it!"

"Pull the damn trigger if you think you're that brave!"

"You got it!"

At the same time that Robert fired the gun, Nicholas exhaled fire onto him. The bullet shot back at him and went through Robert's mouth. There was a huge hole in the back of his head. All of Rene's horrified guests jumped back as he hit the floor.

"You are dead, my brother!" Seth snapped.

"Whatcha gonna do?" Nicholas demanded.

Seth ran to a closet and found an antique sledgehammer that'd been in Rene's dad's family for a long time for generations. When Seth ran outside the closet, Nicholas noticed the sledgehammer and ran from him.

"Why are you running, bitch?"

Nicholas ran up the chimney. Seth climbed up after him. When they got on the rooftop, Seth said, "Don't run; I won't hurt you."

"You're mad, Seth."

"Not mad at all, Nick. I'm furious!"

Nicholas was exhausted as he pulled the sword and watched his brother run toward him with the hammer. He swung it and pounded the side of his head. Nicholas coughed blood and croaked, "See ya in hell!"

Everyone rushed to the hospital and saw that Robert was pronounced dead. Three days later, a funeral was held for him at Jesus of Nazareth Baptist Church, where he attended for fourteen years. He was sadly missed by his family, relatives, and many friends. Nicholas remained missing and missed by no one.

THE 13 STAIRS

At the end of town,
There is a very spooky place.
The cemetery sits on an enormous hill
That has, in front of it, thirteen stairs.
Many people have made dares
After hearing that they'd see Satan's true face.

The townsfolk nicknamed it the "Unholy Trail"
Because it was said to lead to hell.
They said to have seen spirits there in lack of rest
And grotesque demons at their best.

If you go there after sunset,
You can bet
That you're gonna be spooked out
As you see what hell's all about.
When you step to the thirteenth stair,
You'll be on the way to Satan's lair.

When you see the dark-red, winged ghoul,
You will wonder, "How could the inferno be so cruel?"
It will spit at you a million bees
That'll eat you like a cancerous disease.
The stings will leave you bruised and sore.
Then you'll be taken to burn in hell forevermore!

BIZARRE DECEMBER

The sun had just went down
When my friend and I rode into that haunting part of the town.
We felt anything but good
As we went into that neighborhood.

My friend thought, "Halloween's over!
Hell, it's almost time to celebrate our Savior's birth!"
I looked and thought, "What on Earth?"
There was a blue-furred oddball looking like the Sesame Street character
Grover.

He was wearing a brown hat.
Beside him was a large, black cat.
As he talked, his breath smelled like a dill pickle.
In his hand, he held a bloodstained sickle.

Then my friend's car died.
Both of us sighed.
The oddball knew we weren't from there.
He decided to be fair
And tell us of a place to eat
And a hotel down the street.
I told him, "Thank you."
I gave credit where it was due.
After that, he gave us a hundred dollars, several cigars, and a bottle of
wine.
And told us, "Y'all oughta be just fine."

We hurried to the hotel.
My friend and I wondered, "What the hell?"
The lobby smelled like marijuana.
Behind the desk was a purple iguana.
It wore a black suit and tie
As it told both of us, "Hey, big guy."
We wondered, "What the hell?"
The damn lizard sounded female.

I asked it, "Are you woman or man?"
The iguana ignored me and called for the girl who looked like Lindsay Lohan.
The girl led us to Room 607
And told us, "You'll feel just like you're in heaven."

After a while, we went down to the pool.
We thought that it was so cool.
There was the auburn-haired girl having barely anything on.
My friend told me, "Maybe we should leave her alone."

"Hey, y'all," she told us.
We tried not to make a fuss.
I told her, "You must be from the South."
She told me, "Actually, I'm from Innsmouth."
I asked her, "Really?"
She laughed and said, "Don't be silly!"

She told us that she was originally from Baltimore
And that she was almost twenty-four.
She told us that her name was Helena
And laughed, sounding exactly like a hyena.

The three of us talked for an entire hour.
Then she said, "I gotta go clock out for the night. Isn't that sour?"
We went back to our room
And felt doom and gloom.

On the table was an ashtray made of a human skullcap.
My friend leaped for my lap.
We looked outside the window and recognized the full moon.
The antique radio began playing that Zager and Evans tune.
I wondered where my soul would be in ten-thousand years.
I thought, "I need to drink a few cold beers."

I lit up a Marlboro Light
And got my nerves right.
I turned the radio off
And let out a cough.

Hours later was the strike of four
There was a knock on the door.
I reluctantly answered the wakeup call
And saw the oddball.

He looked as if he was furious.

It made my friend and me curious.
He asked, "Why were you hitting on my wife?"
He pulled out the sickle and a butcher knife.

"Y'all were smiting with my woman Helena at the damn pool!"
My friend thought, "You're a damn fool!"
"Y'all don't have to agree. But y'all are both dead!"
I thought, "Enough said!"

My friend and I thought, "We gotta go!"
We jumped out the window.
When we got that far,
We thought, "Damn, that place was bizarre!"

THE DOME-SHAPED HILL

It was early in the month of May
When I walked up the dome-shaped hill late one night.
Then I saw a mysterious beam of light.
It caused me to stare around the hill
And begin to feel
The diabolical presence of they
Whose dark master once tempted Eve
And caused Adam and her to leave
Their beautiful home.
They were the ancient evils dwelling on the hill
In shape of a dome.
Then I began to realize that hell is real!

DEATH'S THRONE

As I walked among the stones,
There were unspeakable chills in my bones.
I felt so alone that night
Because of no soul in sight.
I could hear the sounds of tormented souls
In the endless fires of hell.

After that, I looked at the stone chair
And had a hellish scare.
I began to remember my friend
Who once took a seat in "Death's Throne."

Exactly a year later,
He was laid to rest.
Suddenly, I saw an apparition
Sitting in the chair.
I couldn't believe my eyes!
It was my friend!

He said, "Hello, friend.
I'm so glad you care."
After that, he vanished.
Then I heard Satan calling me
As he was telling me,
"Have no fear.
Take a seat in your ride to eternal death."

FOREST OF 1,000 GHOULS

Journey into the "Forest of 1,000 Ghouls."
Remember the crucifix or holy water as your special tools.
As you walk down to the end of the abandoned lane,
You will enter their hellish domain.

They will bite.
Therefore, be sure you can fight.
The legends are true.
They will seriously harm you.
I guarantee that you'll be frightened to tears
When you see their fiery spears
And you watch them zoom
From the hands of those spirits of doom.

One will feast on your heart
As the others devour your soul apart.
You'll be stone-cold dead.
That's all to be said.

THE GHOSTS OF PALESTINE

I walked into the gates at Palestine
As the autumn weather was so fine.
The time was definitely after nine.

It was half past midnight
As I looked to the gorgeous light
Of the full moon that was so bright.

It was dead silent all around.
Then I heard an eerie sound.
I saw a young woman in a white, bridal gown.
She jogged as she let her brown hair down.
After I watched her vanish into the dark,
I heard a ferocious bark.

I turned to see a Doberman from hell.
When I looked, I could tell
That its eyes were dark-red!

When I stepped back,
There was a faceless nun in black.
She hula-danced around me under the moon.
Then I knew why, at night, Palestine is the most-feared place in the
Yune.

GHOULISH GAMES

I approached the silver gates of "Ghoulish Games" Cemetery
And saw a ghoul so hairy
That it practically looked like an ape with a speared tail.
I felt like I was in hell.
It had horns on its head
And wings that were colored red.

I looked at the ghoul
And thought that it was so cool.
It flapped its wings as it laughed,
"You're a damn fool!"
I felt like I was in a horror story by Howard Phillips Lovecraft.

Then the ghoul explained the reasons that the place got its nickname.
My feelings remained the same.
It told me, "Enter if you dare."
I thought, "I should beware."

Then the after-midnight sky grew blacker than hell!
That was when I heard restless spirits yell.
My brain began to wail,
"Stop abusing me!"
I began to see
The statue that was made in honor of our Redeemer.
It was a helluva beamer
When at least a dozen tarantulas crawled from underneath.

I could no longer be tough.

I thought that I'd had enough.
I ran toward the gate
Until I saw a woman who looked like Fate.
She showed me the blade-sharp point on her wooden cane
And went criminally insane!

When I got back to the gate,
There was the ghoul laughing at how it'd used me as bait.
Out of the blue,
It was the strike of two.
It was a real fright
When I was plucked out of the night
And taken directly to the fiery gate.

There stood the ancient beast
That was awaiting its feast.
It told me that it'd awaited that night since the Stone Age.
I thought that it was an outrage.
I was literally going through hell.
Like Winston Churchill would've told me, I kept going.

THE BLACK WOODS

It was a dark night in late October
When I journeyed into the Black Woods.
The Black Woods were no ordinary woods
For they were supposedly haunted;
Haunted by a witch
Whom everyone proclaimed "one evil bitch!"

The Black Woods were quiet like a mouse
When I found for the house.
I dared myself to walk inside
And thought, "This is like suicide!"
It was made of log
And surrounded by green fog.

I searched for the basement
Where she was said to stay.
I found it and walked down the staircase
Until I saw her hideous face!
She had long, silver hair
And wore a robe of solid black.
Her flesh was wrinkled like a prune
As her nose was warty like a toad.

She cackled as she tugged onto me
As I began begging for my life
I knew I was bound by her evil spell

And bound for hell.
My face turned blue.
I knew what I had to do.
I broke loose from the horrible fiend
And fled the Black Woods,
Vowing to never return!

THE BLOOD FOREST

It was a dark and silent night
When I roamed into the Blood Forest,
Which was a horrific sight.
I thought that it'd be very thrilling
Because it was where Old Man Blood did some stone-cold killing.

Many called him devil-possessed.
That forest was where he worked his best.
With a saw and two knives,
Old Man Blood claimed dozens of lives.

Then in 1926,
The police struck him with their nightsticks
Because they saw him as a little mouse
And committed him to the nuthouse.

It calmed the townspeople's fears
As he was locked away for seven years.
In 1933,
Old Man Blood broke free.
In the forest,
He was killed by a cop.
At age eighty-four,
Old Man Blood was no more.

The time was after midnight
When I got a real fright.
I stared around the place.
Then I saw his face!
He gave me a sinister grin
That was sharper than a shark's fin.
I wanted to cry
When he said, "You're gonna die!"

I felt like a party's uninvited guest.
There were his victims' ghosts
That were the hosts.
They were in lack of rest.
I wanted to faint.
I thought, "This guy makes Ed Gein sound like a damn saint!"

I watched the evil, old man
As his ghost ran.
In the darkness, he disappeared.
I thought that it was very weird.
I began to run as I felt myself burn.
To the Blood Forest, I vowed to never return.

THE HELLHOLE

I don't know what was going on in my brain
When I roamed down St. Luke Lane.
I know when I opened that tunnel's gate,
I didn't feel that great.

I felt as insane as a psychotic loon
When I saw the dark-red, winged baboon
Fly up and cackle like an evil witch.
I thought, "Son of a bitch!"
It said that it'd came for my soul.
Then I knew that I was in a real hellhole.

When I turned back to the gate,
It was too late.
A disfigured midget slammed it shut with a golden lock.
Then he threw a heavy, silver rock.
After that, he laughed, "Face it; you're already dead!"
I saw the blood flow
As the migraine began to grow.
The rising temperature caused me to literally bake
As I was cast into the fiery lake.

THE THIRD BRIDGE

I took a trip down into the woods one night.
Many people told me that the three bridges were a fantastic place for
a good fright.
I walked under the first one
And heard the shot of a gun.
After I walked under the second bridge,
It was very cold.

I roamed under the third bridge.
There he was!
He stared at my face.
Before the Creation,
He was the angel prince of light.
Then he and a third of heaven were cast into that horrible place.
Now, they roam Earth in aggravation.
He roams Earth like a decapitated hen
As he terrorizes lives of women and men.

He grinned and said,
"You've came at the worst time."
I felt like my heart was going to stop on the dime.
He told me that in less than an hour,
I'd be on my deathbed.

The evil one told me that I'd have had a great life
If he would've had his back turned at me.
He said, "A life full of glee."

He told me that I'd have had a gorgeous wife.
He showed her to me on a crystal ball.
She stood at five feet and seven inches tall.
She had long, blond and curly hair
Along with blue eyes making her seem so young and fair.

As I looked into her eyes of such blue,
He told me,
"You had a wonderful future coming to you."
I told him, "I agree."
After that, he laughed and said,
"See you in hell!"
He was gone.
I was alone.
I tried with all my might
To sleep later that night.
Then I kissed life farewell.

WHAT LURKS BEHIND THE ABANDONED CHURCH

On a hill in a small town,
There sits an abandoned church.
Many have went in search
Of what lurks in the graveyard
When the sun goes down.
I guess that they didn't think very hard.

They went through the gate
But never came out.
They were savagely killed.
It made me thrilled
To hear such a bloody story
Of how people went down so gory.

I decided to go and explore.
The place was spooky to the core.
There hadn't been a burial there for over a hundred years.
I felt a hundred fears
When I saw that creature like a red-furred rat.
I thought that it was going to make the Jersey Devil like a pussycat.

It hissed at me like a snake.
That was when I knew that it was from the fiery lake.
It chased me from its dark domain
As the late-night sky poured heavy rain.

A HALLOWEEN NIGHT at WESTMINSTER GRAVEYARD

It was sunset for Baltimore
As the spirits rose from their graves
At the cemetery downtown;
A place infamous as Westminster Graveyard-
Perhaps the most haunted graveyard in the nation
As ghosts roam in aggravation
On the 31st of October,
A night known as Halloween,
When the ghosts make their largest scene
At Westminster Graveyard
Where a visitor stared very hard
And wondered if it was only a hallucination
As they felt the chillingly cold spots
On their back
And saw the colorful orbs in the air
Until he saw a drunk man in black there
As he took him by surprise
And told him,
"Nice to know you care."

Then he vanished into cool air
As the visitor wondered,
"Was Poe ever really there?"
Then the visitor smelled whisky all over the air
As he ran his fingers into his short hair
And looked to the crowded, city street

But felt so alone;
Like the narrator of Poe's most famous work
As he was so weak and weary
On a Halloween Night at Westminster Graveyard.

THE SHUNNED GATE

For over heaven knows how many years
That the people had shunned the gate
That sat at the dead end of the country road.
The legend caused the locals to have unspeakable fears
Of horribly ferocious demons that were full of hate.
It filled their heads with a nightmarish load.

I dared to walk to the gate
As the night got very late.
My nostrils caught a bizarre smell.
I heard the tall tale
Of the demons full of malice
Guarding the gate after sundown.
If anyone came less than fifty feet,
They were escorted to a dark palace.

It was after eleven.
The night grew cool
When I thought of the palace's evil prince
And thought back of the dreadful smell
Because he once said,
"I'd rather reign in hell
Than serve in heaven."
I thought, "What a damn fool!"
That was when I saw someone at the gate
And didn't feel that great.
He was someone whom I didn't want to see.

I saw him there.

He was the infamous prince of the power in the air.

I thought that my heart was going to stop with instant fright

As I had feelings that I was going to be plucked from the night

To be burned and tormented in endless brimstone and hellfire.

For that horrible place, I had no desire.

Therefore, I decided to run away

And shun the gate throughout my day.

AFTERWORD

The model for "Ghoulish Games" Cemetery was Turtleskin Cemetery in my hometown of Picayune, Mississippi. I've heard stories of it being haunted. However, it doesn't have a statue of Jesus as the cemetery in the title poem. There's a statue of our Savior that stands at nearly six feet at the large cemetery at New Palestine Baptist Church, which was practically the setting for "The Ghosts of Palestine." Many people have witnessed the ghost of a woman running with her arms widely out and wearing a white, bridal gown at that cemetery. I've never seen her. I do remember being too far away from the statue and seeing it look just like the Grim reaper. When I was close enough to see what it really was, I was threatened by a dog. I had feelings that it was a hellhound until someone told me that it belonged to people who lived nearby the church.

I told people the story. then I remembered a year before when I was talking with my friend over the phone. I was telling her about touring inside Edgar Allan Poe's house in Baltimore and how Westminster Cemetery(where the author of many brilliantly macabre tales is buried) looks to be a very scary place to be at night. She replied, "Plaxton, I think all cemeteries are a very scary place to be at night!" That wasn't Mindy, to whom I dedicated this book. Mindy and I were elected "Sweetest" of the male and female students at Pearl River Central High School during our sophomore year in November 2003. She and I were very good friends and nothing more throughout high school although I thought she was an absolutely beautiful, young woman.

I really couldn't think of to whom to dedicated this book until I ended up staring at our photo that we took for the 2004 yearbook for PRC High. I was also remembering when I called her months earlier and wished her a happy twenty-first birthday in April 2009. We were discussing memories as well as she told me that I was a good writer. I named the girl in "Eerie October" for my dear friend as well.

The setting for "Eerie October" and "The Diabolical Playground" was Gibson Valley, Mississippi. I believe that Poplarville, Mississippi, was the model for it. It's the seat of Pearl River County and consists of Pearl River Community College, the model for White Mountain Community College in "The House of Gomorrah Falls." I was a student at PRCC for several months in late 2006 until flunking. I ended up working as a client at a vocational rehab facility for months (Dec. 2006-June 2007) in Gulfport, Mississippi, searching for help to find employment. I explained that I'd been diagnosed with Asperger's syndrome in February 2004. I explain it like this; Einstein was brilliant enough to develop the theory of relativity but couldn't comb his own hair. I can remember almost any date in history(e.g. Dec.8, 1980-John Lennon was murdered by deranged fan Mark David Chapman in New York). However, I was in algebra in high school for a third time.

It was around my seventh-grade year at PRC Junior High in late 2000 when I began to amaze my fellow schoolmates with my extraordinary ability. My art teacher was very fascinated with my sketches of such as silent-film comics Charlie Chaplin, Harold Lloyd, and Buster Keaton.

I started my freshman year at PRC High in Carriere, Mississippi, in late 2002. When my English teacher assigned the class to write a story together in groups, most of the class wanted to be in a group; including Alonso from "The Bite of the Bass." That was the first time that I'd written "The Adversary's Son." Months later, I wrote "The Nightmare over Raven's Stone," except it set in a town outside of Boston, Massachusetts. I'd went to the Smoky Mountains in Tennessee at the approximate time. Raven's Stone doesn't exist there as far as my knowledge is concerned. As you may recall, it was the setting for "Ivan and the Stump." What Rebecca Paulsen said at the beginning of that story, I learned that from research on Anton LaVey's point of view on Satan in The Satanic Bible. There was also philosopher Friedrich Nietzsche in nineteenth-century Germany, who refused to believe in a God who wanted praise at all times. HL Mencken, who'd been known as America's answer to Nietzsche, said that a church is where people, who'll probably never make it to heaven, go and listen to a man, who's never been there, tell about it.

I was raised in a Church of God church . I listened to people speak in tongues and fall into the Holy Spirit. I was sixteen when I was baptized in summer 2003. Since that night, I had people ask if I have I'd accepted the Lord Jesus Christ as my Savior. I told that I have. If you can recall, the Bible tells some horror stories. it had to have been scary when God sent the death angel and the horrible plagues in Egypt after the Pharaoh refused to set the Children of Israel free. Then there were the disciples who found the demon-possessed man running naked in the wilderness. For years, no one could stop him until they took him to Jesus. When Jesus asked the man, "What is they name?" He answered, "Legions for we are many!" And how about the stories told in Revelation! Especially in Revelation 13. I challenge you to read it.